JUNKYARD

DOGS

Dave Mills

ISBN 13: 978-1986998109

ISBN 10: 198699810X

In loving memory of Bob and Kathy Kane, my best friend's parents, who were closer to me than my own

FOREWORD

In Junkyard Dogs, David Mills has created a literary portrait of the thoughts and feelings he has experienced in his lifetime battle with the disabling neurological disorder of spinocerebellar degeneration. I met David in grade school when we were 12 years old. He grew up fending for himself and developing the resourcefulness and independence that have served him so well during the decades of pain and obstacles that have confronted him but never defined him. David has been a champion for the rights of the disabled. He has fought to maintain his physical strength and positive attitude through a grueling program of swimming endless miles, for which he has won awards. He may not be able to walk, but he can swim for hours. He has fiercely fought for and defended his own independence and integrity as well as that of others who are affected by disabling disorders. Dave has won the recognition and respect of those who are fortunate to know him and observe his indomitable spirit and impressive accomplishments. He was misdiagnosed with multiple sclerosis. He has endured falls, complications, infections, and setbacks of all types. But he never gives up.

This book is an example of his creativity, energy, and passion.

All of us face adversity in life, but Dave has dealt with more than his share. We can all benefit from his example.

And by the way, enjoy his book!

Tim Kelly, M.D.

TABLE OF CONTENTS

CHAPTER 1

THE JOURNEY BEGINS

The alarm clock buzzed at 4:41 a.m. Tom sat up, reached for the handicap bar on the far wall, and pulled himself into the wheelchair. Once securely in the chair, he turned off the alarm. In the past, he had tried turning off the clock before he was in the wheelchair, but that usually ended up with him falling out of bed.

He started the challenge of getting dressed. To a person without a disability, dressing is an automatic act. For Tom, dressing was the first challenge of many for the day. He had two handicap bars in the bedroom and six in the bathroom, but there was always the possibility of a fall. He moved carefully. His sister always told him he needed to be more spontaneous; however, his world and hers were very different.

After dressing, it was off to fix breakfast. That, too, involved the possibility of danger. Navigating the rather small bathroom was a whole other story!

Somebody knocked at the front door. Students at a local college came by to help him sometimes, but they always called first.

He answered the door and the man introduced himself as Dr. Bob Scott.

Dr. Scott said, "We're having a meeting about the need to continue embryonic stem cell research and we feel you should be there. The meeting is scheduled in Bermuda for the day after tomorrow.

All your travel arrangements will be prepaid, and you will also be paid for your time. This letter explains everything, and I hope to see you there!"

Tom was surprised they wanted him. He asked Dr. Scott if he was the right Tom Emerson, and Dr. Scott assured him that he was.

"The reason I am personally delivering the letter is because we didn't want you to think this was some kind of a scam. You have written several articles in which you stated that you think embryonic stem cell research is necessary. So your input is quite valuable."

"I was only saying what I believe about this issue," Tom said.

After the doctor left, Tom opened the letter, which confirmed everything.

Hi Tom,

We would like you to attend a meeting about stem cell research scheduled for August 4th at 3:00 p.m. The meeting is in Bermuda. Your travel arrangements have been made and paid for. You have reservations for August 4th, with a return trip on August 7th. Your tickets and hotel confirmation are enclosed. You will also be reimbursed for your time.

The handicap van will pick you up on Tuesday, August 4th at 6:15 a.m. When you arrive in Bermuda, you will be met by another attendee, Sue. She will drive you to the meeting.

Sincerely,

Bob Scott, M.D.

As the letter indicated, round-trip tickets to Bermuda and confirmation for a hotel reservation were tucked inside the envelope. Tom had to make a decision. Should he just ignore the letter or accept Dr. Scott's proposal? If he decided to go, he would have to notify the shuttle, airline, and hotel that he would be in a wheelchair. He wasn't sure if he should go, but it was Bermuda after all, so he decided to accept.

"Is that spontaneous enough for you, sis?" Tom said aloud, smiling as he imagined her reply.

Suddenly, he looked at the clock. Dressing and eating breakfast had consumed more than two hours. Tom still had to set up his bus ride for the next day. Even if he went to Bermuda, it would be easy to cancel the ride while also leaving enough time to check emails before he left the house. The computer was the only way he communicated with some people, since he didn't write by hand and his speaking skills were extremely limited.

By 9:00 a.m., Tom's internal clock was calculating how much time he had left to swim. If the bus was on time, he might be able to swim two miles. Swimming was special to him; it was the time when his body didn't hurt, so he could think clearly.

******

Tom woke at 2:00 a.m. The drive took about a half hour. They arrived at the airport at 6:45. They drove past a golf course, where a foursome was playing an early round. It reminded Tom of himself thirty-five years ago, and how he had enjoyed playing golf.

Tom was an average guy. He had planned to get married and have two kids. But life had thrown him a curveball. Over time, his senses were affected. His balance was first to go, so when he played golf he was unable to judge how far he was from the hole. And now he was in a wheelchair.

As Dr. Bob had promised, a Sky Cab helped him to the plane. One good thing about being in a wheelchair: he didn't have to wait long in security lines. But that wasn't much of a tradeoff, since there was always the danger that he would fall and crack his head open.

******

Tom arrived in Bermuda at 1:00 p.m. As soon as he exited the plane, a woman approached.

"Hi, I'm Sue Castleton! How was your flight?"

Tom reached out to shake her hand. "Hello, I'm Tom. It was nice, but I'm not used to riding in First Class."

"Well, we wanted you to be in Row 1 Seat 1, so you didn't have to use the airline's wheelchair. Let's get your luggage and be off."

Tom said, "You know, there was a woman named Sue Castleton who won the 500-meter breaststroke in the 2000 Olympics."

"That would be me! But a lot has happened since then. I only swim a mile a day now. I've already eaten, but if you want, we can stop and get you some food on the way."

******

They stopped at a diner, found a clean booth, and ordered.

Sue said, "I know you have a difficult time talking and eating, so I'll just tell you about the five people you'll meet this afternoon at the meeting. First, there's Monty. He is probably the richest person you'll ever meet. In fact, I think he's one of the top ten richest people in the world.

"Next, there's Dr. Bob, who gave you the letter. I've known him my whole life. He is one of the most caring people I know. Bill…well I don't know much about him. He mostly just talks to Monty. Next is Gabriella; she has a PhD in psychology. She's my roommate and best friend. Her boyfriend used to work with my dad. And finally, there's Dick. He is also in a wheelchair, and he is quite a character.

"I've read your articles on the need for embryonic stem cell research, about how we must embark on this path immediately because people are dying every day, and the fact that this research holds the key to relieving so much so much suffering and hardship. I feel the same way, as do most of the people you will meet today. So many people would still be alive today if we had done more research in the past. I hope you can help us."

CHAPTER 2

THE MEETING

"Good afternoon, everyone. I'd like to begin with introductions. My name is Monty Allen. I graduated from the State University of New York and received my MBA from Harvard Business School. Business has been good to me. I'm president of one of the largest computer companies in the world, and I'm on the board of six foundations. I was married for thirty-six years, but sadly my wife died last year. I have three children: two boys and one girl.

"To my right is Dr. Bob Scott. Bob is the head of neurology at the University of California Medical Center. I will let him talk about his personal history later. Also, I just learned today that he is Sue's godfather.

"To my left is Bill Johnson. Bill retired from the army as a four-star general. He is now president and owner of one of the largest security companies in the world. To Bill's left is Gabriella. She has a PhD in psychology and taught at California State University for ten years. To Bob's right is Sue, my vice president of technical support. If you have any technical questions, she can help you. To Sue's right is Tom, a computer analyst.

"To Gabriella's left is Dick, also known as Deadeye Dick. He stepped on a land mine in Vietnam and received a Medal of Honor. Dick looks like he weighs 300 pounds, but it's all muscle."

Dick had tattoos on both arms. On his right arm was a knife with the word *Betty*; on the left was a dog with the word *Max*. Dick had long, red hair and a beard that had been red at one time but was now mostly gray.

Monty continued. "I'm sure some of you are wondering what this meeting is about. I want to discuss how critical it is that we continue with embryonic stem cell research. As you all know, it is fairly new—we only discovered its importance in 1998. The eight years we just lost during the previous administration was significant.

"The importance of embryonic stem cell research cannot be overstated. Currently, this testing is underway for multiple sclerosis, Alzheimer's, Parkinson's, diabetes, rheumatoid arthritis, and dementia. Significant research is being done with ALS, ataxia, and Friedreich's ataxia. Advancements could mean that the next generation may not have to deal with the emotional and physical pain some of us have dealt with.

"Now I'd like to read a quote by a noted research group. What they say is important, but the wide range of their disciplines is also of great significance."

Stem cells are noted for their ability to self-renew and differentiate into a variety of cell types. Some stem cells, described as totipotent cells, have tremendous capacity to self-renew and differentiate. Embryonic stem cells have pluripotent capacity, able to form tissues of all three germ layers but unable to form an entire live being. Research with embryonic stem cells has

enabled investigators to make substantial gains in developmental biology.

"Some people assume that stem cells from a person's own body will act the same as embryonic stem cells. This is simply not true. Both lines of stem cells have enormous therapeutic potential, but embryonic stem cells offer the potential for wider therapeutic application.

"If you look around the room, each person here has a story. I'd like to share some of mine. I met my wife Sally in college. We were both book-worms. I studied business, and she majored in English literature. My only B in college was in that subject. We were both highly competitive, so one semester Sally said she would take a statistics class if I took an English class. She received an A and I earned a B, a fact she never let me forget. We both graduated within three years. We were boring—a big date for us was running ten miles and then getting a pizza.

"We both went to grad school. After that, we got married and had three children. All my children were runners, because they knew that would probably be the only time they would see me during the day. Work became kind of like a drug to me. I usually worked from eight in the morning until ten at night. On vacation, Sally would only let me turn on my phone for one hour a day.

"Once the kids were in school, she started teaching. But after Sally turned fifty, she started forgetting things. At first, we didn't think much about it. After it got worse, a doctor diagnosed it as early-onset Alzheimer's. The next six years were hell.

"First, she stopped working, then she had to stop driving. It was a hard time. I was lucky: I had

16

Pat and his wife Mary to lean on. By the end, we had to keep an eye on Sally all the time. One time, she put her hand in the fire on the stove. At the end, she didn't remember who I was. I've heard of many people whose loved ones died from Alzheimer's. Sometimes it seems like they're getting better, but then it comes back even worse."

Tom glanced at Gabriella and blushed when she caught him. He noticed she was getting quite emotional.

Monty wiped away a tear. "The doctors tell me that my children may also have the gene for Alzheimer's. The Right-to-Life groups are against embryonic stem cell research. I prefer to think of them as Anti-Quality-of-Life groups instead. They act as if they know the mind of God. Some churches disappoint me—they appear compassionate, yet they let people suffer and die because they believe in fairy tales.

"On November 22nd, there's a protest scheduled where the Anti-Quality-of-Life people will try to stop embryonic stem cell research. The leader and his second-in-command are out to stop stem cell research entirely. I want someone to change their minds."

Monty turned toward Dick's side of the table.

"That's where your talents will be helpful, Dick. I want you and Tom to carry out this task. We have not been totally forthcoming regarding the reason you're here. You both have the option of returning home tomorrow or helping us. Or, if you want, you're welcome to enjoy this nice island for a couple of days and return on Friday. I'm sure you have questions, so let's pause and order dinner. Sam, would you please see what our guests want to eat?"

Sam was dressed in a black suit and referred to everyone formally. He came from a long line of butlers; his father was a butler, as was his grandfather and his father before him.

As Sam asked each person what they wanted to eat, Sue walked over to talk with Gabriella.

Dick approached Monty. "I smoked my last cigarette earlier, and I was wondering if you have any."

Monty replied, "No, but I think Pat might." He signaled Pat to come over and then introduced him as his driver and good friend. Dick asked Pat if he had any cigarettes.

Pat said, "Sure. Do you wanna go out to the back porch and have a smoke?"

Dick said, "That would be great!"

They headed out through the kitchen. Sam was helping a woman prepare the food.

Pat said, "Sam, we're going for a smoke. Can you let us know when the food is ready?"

"Sure, I'll serve you two last. You go out and enjoy your cancer sticks."

Pat laughed. "He's always trying to change me—kind of like my wife. I hope my brand of cigarette is okay."

Dick said, "It's my fucking lucky day, same brand I smoke. You know, I wanted to talk to Bill, ask him he if was ever in 'Nam."

"Mr. Bill fought in Korea and served there for twenty years. I was in 'Nam, too, but didn't get all the medals you got. I was just a young, scared kid. I kept my head down and tried not to get shot."

"Yeah, a lot of guys did that, but I was kind of stupid and thought my country would watch my back." Dick took a drag of his cigarette. "So how long have you worked for Monty?"

"About twenty-five years. Mr. Monty and I go way back. His daughter Amy and my daughter Sandra are best friends. Sandra got married in June, and Amy was her maid of honor. I have a picture—you wanna see it? There's Sandra and Amy, and my other two daughters, Sarah and Cathy, my wife Mary, and Mr. Monty. That was the first time I saw him smile in a long time."

Dick nodded. "You got a fucking nice-looking family."

"Thanks...I think. Are you about done with your cigarette? We should probably go back."

"Sure, I'm getting hungry."

"You go ahead and keep the pack. I have a whole carton in my room."

"That is fucking nice of you, man."

"Uhh, yeah. No problem."

Inside, Sam was preparing dinner for Sue and Tom. "Sir, your dinner will be next. Dick, can you sit down with Pat? Miss Sue and Mr. Monty are talking to Miss Gabriella."

Dick replied, "That would be fine. Pat, can you tell me where you were in 'Nam?"

"Sure, and you can tell me about your medals."

Tom asked Sue, "What were you and Monty talking to Gabriella about?"

She replied, "Gabriella's boyfriend died of early-onset Alzheimer's."

"Oh no. How old was he?"

"He was only forty. Eat your food before it gets cold. I'll tell you more later."

Pat turned to Dick. "To answer your question, I was in Mai Lai."

"That's where I got my first medal."

Pat leaned forward. "Tell me about it."

"I had a small gun and a knife, and I killed six of the enemy before they could kill anyone in my platoon."

Sue whispered to Tom, "It looks like Dick has a friend. They smoked the peace pipe."

Monty tapped on a glass to get everyone's attention. "I imagine you all have many questions."

Dick asked, "What's your plan?"

"We're inventing a way to stop the pro-life leader and his second-in-command—specifically to block their ability to use their kidneys. They'll need to employ other means. Dick, we want to use your knowledge of marksmanship to train Tom."

"Okay. How much does he know about guns?"

"He hunted ducks when he was younger. He also studied wind velocity, which might be useful."

Dick addressed Tom. "Shooting a person is a lot harder than shooting a duck."

Monty continued. "We've been looking at Tom for a long time, and we think he's your man, because in his writing he has stated the importance of embryonic stem cell research."

Dick shook his head. "I know men from 'Nam, and they had what it took—"

Monty interrupted. "You will practice at the rifle range during the day, then hone your skills on a computer simulation for two hours a night."

Dick said, "I see the need for a lot of practice. But go ahead. Tell me more about your plan."

"Bob has developed a pellet that will stop the function of their kidneys so they'll need to have dialysis."

"And how exactly do you expect to get these pellets into their kidneys?"

"You and Tom will a use a small pellet-delivery device. It will need to be at close range, because you must shoot it within two inches of their kidneys."

Dick jerked his thumb at Tom. "Do you think Tommy Boy is up to it?"

"That's your job, and I know you're ready for it."

Dick sat back and folded his arms. "That IS a big job."

"As I said earlier, you both have the right to say no and go home tomorrow."

Dick said, "Sure, and I bet Bermuda has something like the East River where they'll find our bodies."

"I assure you, we are businessmen and not mobsters. No harm will come to either of you."

Dick said, "Let's hope it works. I've had several talks with idiots about embryonic stem cell research. Someone told me they didn't want their tax dollars spent on that or abortion. I replied, 'BOO-fucking-HOO. I didn't want to go to fucking Vietnam, and I sure didn't want to step on a fucking land mine.' Another pro-life jerk said, 'Do you want to kill babies?' I said, 'Talk to me after you spend thirty years in a fucking wheelchair.'"

Monty said, "Dick, you have colorful way of saying what you think. Well, everyone, that's all for tonight. You both have a lot to think about. If you choose to accept this mission, we'll meet back here tomorrow night. Tom and Sue are staying at the Bermuda Hilton, and Dick and Gabriella are staying at the Holiday Inn."

******

On the drive to the hotel, Tom asked Sue, "What do you think about Dick?"

"It's been a long day, so I'll tell you about Dick and Gabriella tomorrow."

Tom had a room with four handicap bars; Sue had the adjoining room.

She said, "I hope everything's all right. I know you have trouble moving around sometimes, so if you need help, just call. Oh, and the pool opens at 7:00 a.m. Want to go for a swim in the morning?"

"Sure."

"Good. I'll get a wake-up call for six if that's all right. Sleep well and we'll talk tomorrow."

Tom replied, "Have a good night."

******

After Sue and Tom ate breakfast the next morning, they went down to the pool. It was a beautiful sunny day.

Tom said, "I usually swim about a mile in an hour and ten minutes." Sue said she was faster.

"It's not an ego boost having a woman swim so much faster than me."

"Well, you know I was a world champion! I've seen several films of you swimming, though. I admire your style."

"You seem to know a lot about me."

"Yes, Monty wanted me to learn all about you. I know about your family members, your school, and your job."

Sue glanced at the large clock on the wall. "It's 7:30, so let's dive in."

She swam her mile in twenty-five minutes.

Tom raised his head from the water. "I'm less than halfway done!"

Sue pulled herself out of the pool to dry off. "That's okay. I need to send some text messages."

After Tom finished swimming his mile, Sue suggested, "Let's go back upstairs and order some lunch, and I'll tell you about Dick and Gabriella."

As they ate lunch in Sue's room, she filled Tom in.

"First, let me tell you about Gabriella. As I told you, her boyfriend was forty years old when he died of early-onset Alzheimer's. They were childhood sweethearts and had planned on getting married the following year. Gabriella's mother had died during childbirth, so she was afraid of having children, plus they both worked a lot.

"Tim was an engineer who worked with my dad. Gabriella's father was a renowned chef. He owned a world-famous restaurant in New York City, where he taught her how to cook. (She makes exquisite food.) Tim's parents visited the restaurant regularly. Tim and Gabriella developed an intimate relationship; they were always together. To no one's surprise, they became lovers. But they were both very involved with their careers.

"Next to Monty, Gabriella is the smartest person I know. Tim's sickness and death were the hardest things she has ever had to experience."

Tom was busy eating, but he listened to Sue intently.

She continued. "You asked what I think about Dick. He was lucky he was in the service, because he sure likes to kill people! If he hadn't been a war hero, I'm pretty sure he would have been a serial killer. He has a knife he calls Betty. When Betty comes out, someone's going to die. Dick actually counts how long it takes them to die.

"Have you ever heard the expression 'junkyard dog'? That's what Dick is like. His dad beat his mom, and they both beat him. Life for him has not been the easiest, and he is a very angry person. Gabriella will have a difficult time controlling his temper."

Tom was not surprised. In the short time he had known Dick, he could tell that he was a very angry person.

******

Later that afternoon, they took the short ride back to the office.

Sue said, "Dinner is a special treat tonight. Gabriella has made London broil; she marinated it all night. You'll never taste anything so exquisite."

Monty greeted them. "The others are already here. Dick is in the weight room showing off his strength."

Gabriella was in the kitchen making dinner. They all went to the gym to watch Dick. After a while, Sam stopped by to tell them dinner was ready.

Monty said, "Before dinner, I'd like to hear your decisions, gentlemen."

Dick gave a thumbs-up. "I'm all in."

"Good. And you, Tom?"

Tom replied, "I've been thinking a lot about how critical it is that we embark on a path toward embryonic stem cell research. My actions will save people's lives, so I'm one-hundred percent with you."

Monty said, "After dinner, I'll tell you the first part of the plan. Enjoy the meal."

******

After dinner, Monty reassembled the group. "Let's review the plan. You're welcome to enjoy this island for a couple of days, but I told a friend I would see her in Miami tomorrow night. After a couple of days, I want you to join me there. Tom and Sue, I found a house with a swimming pool where you can swim laps. Dick and Gabriella, you will stay two doors down, in a house with a gym where Dick can work out. Pat has even offered to come over each morning to spot you.

"As I said earlier, during the day, you guys will go to the rifle range. The women will help plan our activities. And at night, Sue will train everyone. Any questions?"

Dick whined, "I need to take orders from the girls?"

Monty replied, "Get used to it! If there are no more questions, then that's all for tonight."

******

When Sue and Tom returned to the hotel, it was about nine o'clock.

As they moved through the lobby, Tom said, "According to Monty, we all have a reason we are involved in this mission. What's yours?"

"My dad died from ALS. He and Mom knew about it for months before I swam at the 2000 Olympics, but they didn't tell me until after I'd won the gold medal. When you win all your meets, you don't think about how much your parents sacrificed. Dad wasn't a rich man, but he and Mom came to all my meets. If it was far away, he would buy airplane tickets for me and Mom. He would work four ten-hour days, then drive all night to see me swim. He spent all his vacation time at my meets.

"Most mornings, Mom would wake me before 5:00 a.m. to drive me to practice. I was their only child, so everything was about me. After the 2000 Olympics, I wanted to give them the vacation they

34

always wanted, but instead my dad spent two months in the hospital.

"At the funeral, there were a lot of tears, but the people who cried the deepest were my mom, myself, and Dr. Bob. He was my dad's closest friend, the best man at my parents' wedding, and my godfather. My mom died the next year. They said it was a heart attack, but I always suspected it was from a broken heart. I don't think I'll ever recover…"

Sue started to cry. Tom gave her a hug.

"Tom, can I sleep here tonight? I don't want to be alone."

They held each other tight and enjoyed the closeness.

Sue snuggled in and whispered, "Tomorrow, after our swim, it's time for you to tell me your story."

******

After lunch the next day, Sue said, "Okay, let's hear it. What's your story?"

Tom said, "Well…I haven't had a girlfriend in forty years. (Don't worry—this isn't a pity party.) I was always kind of a square peg that didn't fit in a round hole. At a very young age, I was different. I had two brothers and two sisters. They were all into sports. My dad and mom supported them with great joy. After high school, my sisters married guys who were also jocks. Their husbands worked at the factory, and they had kids who were also into sports. My brothers took pretty much the same path.

"I was the strange one. I liked math and not much else. I liked girls, but they usually just saw me as a friend. My friend Don always won any girl he wanted. One time, his girlfriend got mad about his womanizing, so she decided to sleep with one of his friends. Even though she and I were very close, she found someone else to be her partner. I always wondered if that was because my family was working-class, or maybe it was because the doctors had started talking about my multiple sclerosis. I guess I'll never know.

"After college, my career was the only thing I could count on, and my health issues were always a concern. After my company decided I should take disability leave, swimming became my whole life. I hear similar stories from a lot of people with disabilities.

"Life can be a challenge, but embryonic stem cell research can give us a shot at healthier lives. I just don't understand why Anti-Quality-of-Life people want to take that opportunity away from thousands of people with disabilities."

******

Thoughts From the Author

Here, I would like to discuss three groups that embryonic stem cell research would benefit. They overlap somewhat, but all three need to be mentioned.

The first group is famous people like Christopher Reeve, who might still be alive today if we had researched his condition more. We are more knowledgeable about the solar system thanks to Stephen Hawking, who has ALS. Montel Williams, who has MS, has inspired millions of people. So has Michael J. Fox, who has Parkinson's. These men have made the planet a better place, and there are many people who would benefit, live longer, and inspire others.

The second group is regular people who have worked their whole lives but now must deal with a disease such as Parkinson's, MS, or ALS.

A group of scientists from the University of New South Wales says a new cell technique has the ability to not only regrow bone and tissue and heal wounds, but also to create more complex structures and organs.

However, many religions believe abortion is a sin, plain and simple. A pro-lifer would say it's acceptable to use stem cells from a person who has died from natural causes, but not embryonic stem cells, because they are sacred.

But what about ME? There are several problems with using stem cells from a person who has died. A pro-lifer will never admit they are wrong, no matter how many people die. A friend of mine had a successful stem cell implant and she is very grateful. She prays every night to thank the fetus who gave her a second chance at life. Is a fetus more important than a person who is already alive?

The Anti-Quality-of-Life people would say she killed a child. I think we need to think the matter through more carefully. For many years, it was pro-life versus pro-choice, but with embryonic stem cell research, things have changed. What if, with a realistic view of abortion, we might save hundreds of lives? So I see pro-life as the furthest thing from improving the lives of thousands or maybe millions of people. Maybe the time has come for us to see abortion not as sin but as a gift to help people.

******

Tom said, "I often wonder how things might have been different if that girl in college had thought I was worth knowing. I have so much love that has never been shared. I'm going to die soon, and the only thing my gravestone will say is HE WAS A NICE GUY."

Sue hugged and kissed him gently.

"You might want to take a little nap. Dick and Gabriella will be here in a few hours."

"Where are we going for dinner?"

"The hotel restaurant—it has the best lobster on the island."

******

Dick and Gabriella arrived right at 5:30.

Dick commented, "Gabriella, you don't drink? That's okay—more for me!"

Gabriella laughed and asked the group, "Can you believe Dick likes the Philadelphia Eagles? You know, the team that had a dog killer as a quarterback and took 87 years to win a Super Bowl?"

Gabriella was a petite woman, yet her feelings about football were comparable to that of most men.

Dick replied, "Do you know she likes the Dallas Cowboys? Everything in Texas is big...and that includes big egos!"

She said, "You should know!"

******

When Sue and Tom returned to their hotel, she admitted, "I have a confession. Monty didn't want us to meet until yesterday because he was afraid it might influence your decision. So he had me look into your background. I've been studying everything about you. I know your childhood, your college life, your career, and your illness. I even knew about that college girl you mentioned.

"Before I met you, I came to respect you a great deal. Now that we've met, I'd really like to get to know you better. I hope you feel the same..."

"Definitely," Tom replied.

They fell asleep holding each other once again.

The next day was their last on the island. They had a short swim, then headed to Florida.

CHAPTER 3

FLORIDA

The four of them flew to Florida. They traveled
First Class. It was only a twenty-minute flight. Dick
was excited because he did not have to pay for
any drinks. Gabriella and Sue talked endlessly
about things women talk about. Tom sat back and
relaxed. Sometimes, he looked at Sue and she
smiled.

When they got to Miami, Sue got a text from Monty telling her what was waiting for them outside. After they got their luggage, they headed out front and saw a big white van with a lift and places for two wheelchairs. It even had hand controls for the handicapped.

Gabriella drove, and Sue got another text message from Monty.

"The GPS has been set up to guide you to your temporary homes."

First, they drove to the house that Sue and Tom would share. It was a nice one-story ranch with two bedrooms, completely wheelchair accessible, with a twenty-five-meter lap pool.

The place that Dick and Gabriella would share was just a couple houses away. It was also a ranch with three bedrooms. The house included a large gym for Dick and a yoga room for Gabriella. It had an enormous TV in the den. Dick had requested that all the phones have extra-large buttons since he had such large hands.

That night, Gabriella made one of her great dinners— roasted duck in orange sauce over white rice and a fresh salad.

******

On the way over to Gabriella and Dick's house the next morning, Tom said to Sue, "I felt bad waking you up so early this morning. Could you please ask Monty if someone could put handicap bars in the other room, so I can dress in there?"

When they arrived at the house, Gabriella was busy putting dinner in the crockpot.

Tom said, "Gee, Gabriella, I wish we could help with the food."

Sue said, "Gabriella always cooks. When she lived with me, she was meticulous and said I would make it wrong."

Tom said, "I want to share the chores. So if you make the food, I should do the laundry."

Gabriella said, "Great, that would be nice. But one thing: you must wash and dry your and Dick's clothes together. Sue's and my clothes must be washed separately, because I hate the smell of tobacco smoke. I tried to get Dick to take a shower after his workout, but he never showers in the middle of the day."

So while they stayed in Florida, Tom was in charge of the laundry; the only thing he would let Sue do is fold her and Gabriella's clothes.

Gabriella said, "I'm glad we have a privacy fence, because Dick was out back earlier showing

Pat the right way to throw Betty so he could kill someone quickly."

After she finished preparing the chicken, she said, "We should go."

When Dick saw Tom's shorts, he said, "Looks like you're dressed for the beach, not the gun range!" He made Gabriella promise to buy Tom some jeans.

Sue said, "Tom, Monty said you and Dick are going to the shooting range and we should come to the office. He also said there's a hamburger place on the way. You and Dick might want to get lunch, because you won't be eating again until dinner. A friend of Monty owns the place—it's called Big Al's Shooting Range. Big Al was a guard for the Miami Dolphins for ten years. Also, a friend of Dick runs it."

******

Tom had his misgivings about spending the whole day with Dick. He was like the boss no one liked. When they got to the shooting range, the manager greeted Dick.

"You old crazy son-of-a-bitch. What the fuck are you doing here?"

Dick was a legend in certain circles. He had won every rifle shooting contest for the past thirty years, and he had even tried to plan a knife-throwing event. It was an event he would probably also win at the para-Olympic games.

Dick said, "I'm here to teach this guy Tommy Boy how to shoot."

The manager was known as Good Old George. He was friendly with Dick, but also aware of his foul temper.

Good Old George said they were welcome to have a cold beer when they were done. Tom and Dick started to practice.

Dick said, "We'll start with a target fifty yards away."

Tom was shaking, with sweat dripping off his head. He took a deep breath before his first attempt, but only hit the paper target's right leg.

Dick said, "You'll have to do better than that. Here, let me show you how it's done." He shot and hit the target in the heart. He tried to show Tom how to aim the rifle. His next shot was a little better, but still not great.

Dick said, "This is going to take a lot of work."

They practiced all day. Each time, Tom would do a little better, but Dick shook his head, and started throwing things on the ground, yelling, "I'm training a boy, not a man!"

At four o'clock, Dick said, "We better stop for today, because it's looks like it's going to rain soon."

They headed back to the office, which had a small covered porch with two tables and assorted chairs. They went into the office, where George was helping a customer.

After he was done, he asked, "You ready for that beer, Dick? How about your friend?"

Dick said, "That wimp only drinks soda."

George said, "All I have is Coke."

Tom nodded. "That's good."

Dick said, "How much do we owe you?"

George said, "Your money's no good here."

Dick pulled out a cigarette.

George said, "The fucking law says we can't smoke in here. Do you wanna go outside?"

They sat at a small table near the door, so George could see the office.

"So who do you fellas like in the Super Bowl?"

Dick said, "I think Denver has a shot. And there's always the Eagles."

Finally, when it had stopped raining, Dick said, "We should be off, but we're coming back tomorrow."

George said, "You want a beer for the road?"

Dick said, "Sure. Tommy Boy, you're too slow. I'm gonna go ahead and enjoy my beer and cigarette."

As Tom headed for the parking lot, he heard Dick shout, "Move that piece of shit before I come over and cut off your balls!" He started to pull Betty from his boot.

Tom yelled, "Put that thing away, Dick!"

The guy was driving a big black Hummer. He weighed about 300 pounds, and there was a young woman sitting next to him.

Tom said, "Could you please move your car? We're gonna need that handicap space in a couple minutes..."

He replied, "Since you asked nicely, sure I'll move."

Dick said, "You better—before I come over there and make you!"

Just then, Sue and Gabriella drove up, in time to see the guy move and Dick yelling at him. Sue hurriedly helped Tom into the van, and whispered loudly to Dick, "Monty said we should keep a low profile!"

On the ride back to the houses, they mentioned the problems Dick had had in New Jersey.

Tom asked, "What problems?"

Sue said, "I'll tell you later."

Dick shouted, "That guy was being a real asshole! He never should have parked in the handicap space."

Gabriella said, "Would it kill you to ask him to move?"

"I DID ask him."

Tom said, "I think you TOLD him."

Dick said, "You guys are just wimps."

Gabriella said, "Are you trying to get us killed? Who do you think you are, Keyser Söze?"

"Who the hell is that?"

"A character in *The Usual Suspects*. That was a great movie."

Dick said, "I bet you'll text Monty about that incident."

"I already have, and he wants to have a video conference tonight."

"Good. Maybe he'll understand my feelings."

******

Back at the house, Gabriella said, "I'll fix dinner. You guys should take showers. You both smell terrible!"

Tom and Sue walked next door to get ready for dinner. While Tom showered, Sue went online. She had taken a picture of the Hummer's license plate. After some research, she discovered it was a dealer plate, and the guy worked at a used-car dealership in town. She texted Monty.

He texted back, "You go and have dinner, and I'll take it from here."

After his shower, Tom said, "Earlier you mentioned that Dick had an incident in New Jersey. Could you tell me more about it?"

"Dick had a fight with a guy and killed him. Gabriella has the court hearing on DVD. I can play the recording tomorrow morning if you'd like."

"That would be good."

******

Gabriella announced dinner proudly, like an artist presenting her work. "We're having chicken cacciatore and antipasto."

Dick said, "I'll have the chicken stuff, but I don't want any salad."

Gabriella said, "I will consider it an insult if you don't try my antipasto salad."

Dick said, "I don't like rabbit food."

Sue said, "Try it. Gabriella doesn't make food that isn't delicious."

Dick agreed to have some just to keep Gabby happy. As it turned out, he liked the taste. They all enjoyed the dinner.

After dinner, Dick said, "I'm going to have a smoke."

Gabriella said, "Remember, Monty wants to talk to us at 7:30."

Tom told the women about their target practice.

Gabriella said, "You listen to Dick. He may be a jerk, but he knows about guns." Sue was interested to hear how Tom had dealt with the guy in the Hummer.

At 7:30, they all sat down to watch Monty on the video monitor.

"First, I want to remind all of you, but mainly Dick: we want to keep a low profile. So you should not shout at people who park in handicap spaces."

Dick said, "That guy was being an asshole."

Monty said, "I agree. We found out that he works for a used-car dealership. It turns out the owner's mother is also in a wheelchair, so he will

58

be fired tomorrow for parking the company's van in a handicap space. But when a person parks in a handicap space without a sticker, you should not DEMAND that they move."

Dick reluctantly said, "Okay."

Monty said, "Now to get on with other business. On October 22nd, our targets will be visiting a hospital burn ward. When they exit the ward, they will pass by the nurses' station. We have someone on the inside who told us the Anti-Quality-of-Life leader, Mr. Peters, will use the elevator while another person, Mr. Cooper, will use the stairs.

"Mark will ask for their autographs. That's when Dick and Tom will shoot dart guns that look like straws, which will inject the men with a serum to infect their kidneys. Gabriella and Sue will push you guys into a room and lock the door. You will head for the closet, which has a firefighter pole that goes to a lower floor. Pat and four of my other friends will be waiting there to help you.

"I know this is a lot to remember, but you will practice it many times over the next three weeks. Are there any questions?"

Dick said, "This plan seems to depend on short-range targets, so why are Tommy Boy and I going to the rifle range every day?"

Monty said, "We hope this works, but more drastic action may be required, so we want to be prepared. If there are no more questions, you'll probably want to get some sleep, because it will be a long couple of days."

When Sue and Tom returned to their house, Sue said, "Monty got you a present. He noticed you are having a hard time keeping up, so he bought this new wheelchair. It's not totally powered, but the wheels have little motors on them, so they require little effort to move you."

They went to bed, and Sue was even more passionate than before. She remarked how proud she was of the way he had handled the situation with the guy in the Hummer.

"Dick's a scary guy—that took a lot of nerve to tell him to put Betty away. I'll show you the video tomorrow, and you'll see how bad his temper can get."

They had wonderful sex.

******

The next morning, Sue set up the video and told Tom they would only have time to swim a half mile. "The video shows only the highlights of a trial that lasted four days; we condensed it to forty-five minutes."

The state was prosecuting Dick on man-slaughter charges. Dick was annoyed by the situation and wondered—since the fight was between two men and he was the victor—why the law was getting involved.

The first witness was a friend of the victim. The prosecutor asked a man named Mr. Scott to describe what had happened on the night in question.

Mr. Scott said, "The defendant started a fight with my friend over a football game. Then he beat him to death."

The prosecutor asked, "Since the defendant is in a wheelchair, why didn't your friend just run away?"

"My friend and the defendant agreed to be tied together with a rope about four feet apart when they fought."

"How many times did your friend hit him?"

"Not once—the defendant broke both his hands. I think he was on some kind of drugs."

The prosecutor said, "I have no more questions."

The judge looked at the defense attorney. "Your witness, Mr. Barnes."

Mr. Barnes said, "Isn't it true that the police tested my client for drugs and only found alcohol in his system?"

"I think the test was rigged. What kind of man can grasp another man's hand and crush all the bones?"

"Didn't your friend say he would put Dick in the hospital?"

"He was just joking."

"No further questions, Your Honor."

The prosecutor said that would be his last witness.

Mr. Barnes said, "The defense would like to call Senator Clem."

After Senator Clem was sworn in, he was asked, "What is your occupation, sir?"

"I am a Republican senator from West Virginia."

"And how do you know the defendant?"

"We fought together in Vietnam."

"Did you ever witness an incident similar to the one we just described?"

"Yes. Some Viet Cong had captured four Americans and shot one member of our team. Dick swung his arms and broke one of the soldier's wrists, making him drop his gun. Then Dick broke the guy's other hand. He hit him in the head at least five times. Then he used the guy's body as a shield and picked up the gun. After that, the other Viet Cong ran away. Then Dick made a loud call, which he claims is his 'junkyard dog' yell."

Mr. Barnes said to the prosecutor, "I have no more questions. Your witness."

The prosecutor asked, "Senator, would you call Dick your friend?"

"Yes. He saved my life. Dick may seem gruff, but he is a very nice guy. I have seen him three times in the last forty years. We tried to hold a reunion, but no one wants to talk about the war."

The prosecutor said, "No further questions."

The judge said, "If the defense has no more witnesses, I would like to hear closing arguments tomorrow."

The recording cut to the next morning. The prosecutor said to the jury, "It's not unusual to hear about a bar fight, but the defendant is an extremely angry and dangerous person."

Sue paused the tape. "The prosecutor said a lot of other stuff, but we all know Dick is crazy." She hit Play again.

The defense attorney spoke to the jury. "In war, soldiers must picture the world as a place to kill or be killed. Sometimes it's hard to turn these instincts off once the soldier is back home. The defendant has six medals, including a Purple Heart and a Medal of Freedom. To put him in jail would dishonor this man who fought for our country."

It only took an hour for the jury to come back with a verdict of Not Guilty. The judge said he agreed with the verdict, on the condition that Dick see an anger management counselor.

******

On the way over to Gabriella and Dick's house, Tom tested his new wheelchair and seemed impressed how easily it moved. By the time they arrived, Pat had already left. Gabriella was putting meat loaf in the crockpot.

Dick said to Tom, "Looks like you got some new wheels. Maybe now you can move faster."

Their routine was the same as the day before. Dick and Tom went to the rifle range, while Gabriella and Sue went to the office.

On the drive to the range, Tom said, "I saw a video about your trial."

Dick said, "It was all bullshit. My lawyer wanted to put in the stuff about me being a soldier so the jury would buy it."

When they got to the rifle range, Dick said, "Good Old George was at the trial, plus he was at the bar."

He asked George, "Do you remember when they tried me for that manslaughter charge? Do you think my being a soldier affected anything?"

George said, "No, you're just a crazy son-of-a-bitch. You also made that guy pretty mad yesterday."

Dick said, "What guy?"

"That big guy who drives the Hummer. I think they call him Big Mike."

"Oh, that fat fuck. I don't think you'll see him for a while."

"Why, what did you do?"

"Nothing, but he got fired."

On the way to the firing range, Tom asked, "Did you ever see an anger management counselor?"

Dick said, "Yeah, but all he wanted was someone to help him get pot! He tried to get me to use the stuff. He said it would mellow me out. I told him that it wasn't for me."

At the end of the day, on the way to the parking lot, Dick said, "You think you're hot stuff with that new wheelchair. I bet I can beat you in a race."

So off they went as fast as they could. Dick won, but he spilled his beer, and howled his junk-yard dog yell. It was strange to see a grown man bellowing like a dog, but Dick was not your average guy. Gabriella and Sue had already pulled into the parking lot, so there was no time for him to smoke.

******

Dick loved the meat loaf.

Gabriella said, "If there's any extra, you can use it for sandwiches tomorrow."

Tom asked, "Can you make one for me also?"

When Dick returned from his after-dinner smoke, Sue shared, "We have some new helpers."

There was a knock at the door. Pat introduced the three men. The tall one with blond hair was Mark; the other two, with muscular builds, were Stuart and Nat.

Sue handled the group introductions. "Tonight, we want to do a trial run to show you our plan." She turned to Tom and Dick. "Tonight and tomorrow night we'll use a hologram to display exactly where the kidneys are located. On the night of the attack, Gabriella and I will be in disguise, and there will be no talking. A machine that fires blank bullets will be used.

"So, Dick, are you ready?"

"Of course." Dick was calm and aware of his ability. He raised his head and shot the blowgun with masterful precision.

Dick and Gabriella did everything exactly as planned.

Sue said, "After Dick uses his blowgun on Mr. Peter, someone will use one on the bodyguards to knock them out for a while. We will then use a machine to shoot blanks. In all the confusion, Gabriella will push Dick into a hospital room and lock the door. Then they will use the pole to make their escape.

"Then it will be Tom's and my turn. The only difference is that Tom will deal with Mr. Cooper, who will be using the stairs. Tom, after you slide down the pole, you'll land on a mat and crawl out of the way. I'll be right after you and can help you get into the other wheelchair."

After they had practiced, Sue said, "That's all for tonight. Are there any questions?"

No one responded. "Good. Tomorrow night, we'll do the same thing."

******

Later that night, Sue told Tom, "Monty wants you, me, and Gabriella to wear necklaces he calls the Dick Alert System. If Dick starts any trouble, like with the guy in the Hummer, we can press the button to alert him immediately.

"He also wants Gabriella and me to take kick-boxing classes, which start tomorrow. The classes are from three to four o'clock on Thursday, so Pat will pick you up from the rifle range on those days. Dick is not allowed to smoke in the van though. Oh, and when you get home, the handicap bars will be in the extra room, so you can get dressed in there."

******

The following day, things were different between Tom and Dick. They seemed to be almost friends.

Dick said, "I know why you've been a lot happier the last couple of days—you got laid!"

Tom said, "You make everything sound so crude."

"I used to think there were only two reasons I ever got laid. Either a woman felt sorry for me, or she wanted to sleep with a Medal of Honor winner. But Gabriella showed me a third reason. She wants to control me—and it works."

They greeted Good Old George.

He asked, "Kill anybody last night, you crazy old-son-of-bitch?"

Dick said, "Maybe you—tonight!"

As they headed for the range, Tom asked, "What disability does George have exactly? He looks fine to me."

Dick said, "Did you notice you never see George wear shorts? That's because he was a victim of Agent Orange, and his legs are all scarred up."

After they had drinks with George, Pat was waiting in the parking lot.

Dick said, "Did you hear Tommy Boy got laid the past two nights?"

Pat said, "I heard that, and Gabriella has slept with you all but two nights."

Tom said, "Really?"

Pat said, "At our meeting the other day, she said she didn't need a PhD in psychology to know how to control your anger. Monty agreed. He said his wife did that to him once, and he responded the same way. We all got a big laugh out of that."

Pat said, "Gabriella is a beautiful woman…"

Dick said, "I know, and when this is over, she will move on."

******

Gabriella had dinner ready. She announced her creation: Hungarian stew with homemade bread. As usual, everyone loved it. While Sue cleaned the dishes, she asked about everyone's day.

"Dick seemed happier with my shooting today."

Gabriella said, "Good, then there were no more incidents?"

Tom said, "No, he was fine."

When Pat and his friends arrived, Dick came back inside.

Sue said, "For our first night, Monty was fairly happy with the way things went. Bill said we should improve our time, though. He also suggested we open a hospital window, so they think we escaped that way."

"Remember, tonight's the last night you'll have the hologram showing you where to aim. So make special note of where to fire. We'll practice everything three times tonight."

******

On the way back to the other house, Tom asked Sue, "Why do you call Gabriella by her full name, but Dick calls her Gabby sometimes?"

Sue said, "Gabriella loved two men in her life, and they always called her by her full name. Her father was a very important person in her life. After school, he introduced her to the art of making great food. On weekends, they would watch sports on

TV, and sometimes he would take her to football games. Unfortunately, he died in his fifties. Tim was the second love of her life, and he always called her Gabriella. The reason Dick calls her Gabby is the same reason he calls you Tommy Boy. He's just being Dick."

******

The next morning, Sue woke at 6:30 and decided to try some different strokes, a half-mile backstroke and half-mile butterfly.

When she was done, Tom said, "Looking good!"

Sue started to cry, and he wheeled over to her. "Oh sweetie, what's wrong?"

"Once my father told me about his ALS, swimming seemed less important, and when my mother died, I almost stopped completely. Only in this last year have I been able to swim a mile. Now with your love, I feel stronger."

"You're a beautiful person, inside and out."

"Thank you, Tom. You're making life worth living again."

******

At the main house, Gabriella said, "I noticed a billboard that reads VOTED BEST PIZZA IN FLORIDA. What do you guys think?"

Sue said, "Let's try it."

Dick said, "Pizza! Something normal finally."

On the way to the rifle range, Gabriella asked the guys, "What do you like on your pizza?"

They both said, "Sausage and pepperoni."

"Do you like extra cheese?"

They both said, "Yes!"

"Sue and I like mushrooms and green peppers. So we'll get two large pizzas. We will stop at lunch and buy fresh veggies."

Dick said, "I thought you were getting pizza from that place."

Gabriella said, "I am, but I like my pizza half cooked, and then I add my own ingredients."

"Why?"

"It's a lot better."

Dick said, "I guess."

******

George greeted them at the range. "Good morning. How are you doing, you crazy son-of-a-bitch? Tom, you get an award for spending so much time with Dick."

Dick said, "You ever had pizza from that place down the road?"

"Sure, they have the best fucking crust and sauce I ever had."

"I guess we'll have that for dinner tonight."

"I hope you did your workout this morning, because you're probably gonna eat a lot tonight. You want your usual rifles?"

"Nope. A friend gave us new ones. They are fucking nice guns. You wanna see them? They are Model 92s, Winchester/Browning/Rossi/Navy. They are very precise, and they cost $20,000 each."

Good Old George whistled, ran his hands along the side of one, aimed it, and smiled. "These are nice!"

Dick said, "Tommy Boy needs better aim, so I'm gonna increase his distances today."

Tom's aim had improved dramatically; every time Dick increased the distance, Tom hit his target.

******

On the way home, Sue said, "Monty wants to talk with us at 7:30 and then we can see *The Usual Suspects*."

Gabriella said to Sue, "Next weekend, football season starts. You know what that means…"

Sue said, "Yes, nothing but football the whole weekend. I'm glad I have Tom to keep me company."

Dick said, "Football every weekend sounds good to me."

After dinner, Monty reported in. "We are all fairly happy with the progress you made this week, but next week is essential, so get some target practice this weekend. What movie are you going to see tonight?"

Gabriella said, "*The Usual Suspects*."

Monty said, "Great movie! There's a lot of violence in that one—Dick should be real happy. Enjoy it, and I'll see you all Monday."

Everyone loved the movie, and Dick had a new hero in Keyser Söze.

Gabriella said, "I've always heard great things about South Street. Can we go there?"

Sue said, "Sure, lots of places to shop."

Dick said, "I hear they also have great bars."

Gabriella said, "It's settled. We'll see you at about ten o'clock. Is that okay?"

Sue said, "That's fine. Tom is swimming a mile and a half tomorrow."

On the way home, Sue said, "I'm glad Dick liked the movie, because some Fridays we'll pick movies he might not like so much."

Sue and Tom had another wonderful night together.

******

The next morning, after Tom was done showering, he found Sue in the living room texting.

"Monty says he wants someone to stay with Dick all day, so when Gabriella and I go to the shops, you and Dick should go to a restaurant bar. Try to get him to pace his drinking, because we're going to dinner with old friends of Gabriella who own the restaurant. Also, he said we are staying at a hotel tonight, so pack an overnight bag."

On the walk over to the main house, Sue gave Tom $300 in cash. "Monty wants us to use one credit card in the name of a business friend. If you have any credit cards, cut them up, because he wants us to be very security-minded."

It was a long drive from Fort Lauderdale to South Street.

Along the way, Gabriella said, "When we were getting ready, Dick had another crazy outburst—you know, the kind where his face turns as red as his hair."

Sue said, "Oh no. What happened?"

"I had the news on. This stupid commercial came on, and he started screaming for me to change the channel. He said the woman was the 'queen bee' of the Anti-Quality-of-Life movement. That her philosophy was that if you're not a whole person, you're fucked. Then he went on about the furniture she was trying to sell. She said it made you feel like warm hands were wrapped around you. He said the only time he felt warm hands was when his father had put his hands around his throat. After a while, he finally calmed down."

Tom and Sue started laughing.

Dick said, "I didn't want to end up in a wheel-chair, but that bitch is more interested in unborn children than helping me."

Gabriella said, "We're having dinner with very dear friends of mine tonight. It's a seafood place, so no whining about the food, Dick. Sue and I will have stone crabs. They also have a great tilapia."

Dick said, "What's tilapia?"

Sue said, "It's whitefish with no bones."

Gabriella said, "I have some good news to share. Next Saturday, the University of Southern California will play Notre Dame. I'm a proud graduate of USC and taught there for ten years. Dick, who was raised Catholic (I know it's hard to believe), decided we should have a bet. Since money is not very significant to either of us, we decided to make our wager about a task the other person must complete. We have until Thursday to decide what that task will be for the loser. So we'll be asking both of you for your suggestions."

Finally, Gabriella turned onto South Street. "Sue and I are going to do some shopping. I'm sure you guys would be bored to death. So you're welcome to go hang out at a restaurant and we'll meet you later. Monty texted me this morning, and since our dinner doesn't start until seven, he reserved a couple of rooms for us at a local hotel. We'll drive back tomorrow morning."

******

While Gabriella was trying on a red dress, she asked Sue, "Can you think of a task Dick can do when he loses our bet?"

Sue said, "Maybe he can stop smoking for week."

"I don't think that would work. When a person stops smoking, they get grouchy. Dick's already a jerk, and we don't want him to be worse!"

Sue laughed. "Maybe you can get him to stop drinking for a week?"

Gabriella said, "We all know that will never happen." They laughed again.

They both bought a few things and walked across the street. They were dressed nicely for dinner.

Sue said, "You know, we have to get Dick and Tom to buy some new clothes. I don't think Tom will mind that much, but it will be a different story with Dick. Oh! I know. For the bet, you should make Dick dress up in women's clothing, come down here, and walk up and down this street a few times!"

Gabriella laughed and said, "He would be an ugly woman! Let's look at some dresses."

******

Back at the restaurant, Dick said to Tom, "You guys all have these fancy degrees. You know, I went to West Virginia Community College for four years. It was on Uncle Sam's dime, and I sure got laid a lot. I got a degree in physical therapy. People said nobody would hire a physical therapist in a wheelchair, but I didn't care. I had a small apartment near the gym and a good local bar. The government paid for that, too."

They ordered lunch and ate in silence. Then they headed over to the park to meet the women.

Tom said, "It's only 1:30. Aren't we going to be early?"

Dick said, "I want to smoke, and there will be plenty to look at."

******

Gabriella and Sue were still shopping.

Sue said, "Aren't you worried we'll be late?"

Gabriella said, "No, Dick will have a smoke and he won't mind checking out the ladies. I thought of a task for him if he loses the bet. He'll have to go to the gay beach and get a guy to want him!"

Sue said, "Any guy would have to be crazy to fall for Dick."

"You're probably right, but it's still funny. Time to find Dick some clothes."

******

Back at the park, Dick was checking out all the women in bikinis.

"Sue has a cute little figure. Does she ever wear a bikini?"

Tom said, "No, bikinis aren't for swimming, they're for looking good."

******

Gabriella and Sue met up with the guys at the park at 1:45.

Gabriella said, "Now we have to find you some decent clothes for tonight."

Dick said, "These are fine."

Gabriella said, "No, you need something better for tonight."

They found a shop with nice men's shorts and shirts.

Gabriella said, "All you need are some quality shorts and an Izod shirt."

Tom said, "No problem."

Dick complained.

******

Gabriella suggested, "Let's go to the hotel and rest up. We're staying at a place I know well. I came down to Florida every January when my dad was alive, and every spring break with Tim."

She was surprised to recognize the guy at the reservation desk. "Hi, Pete! I'm surprised you haven't retired by now."

Pete said, "I enjoy my job, so I'll be here until they make me retire." He typed in their reservation information. "I took my wife to Mr. Jason's restaurant last year for our anniversary. He told us about Tim. I was sorry to hear that he passed. He was a great guy."

Gabriella said, "Thank you. I still miss him. These are my friends—Sue, Tom, and Dick. We're having dinner with Jason and Dallys tonight at seven, so we're going to rest for a while."

Pete said, "Do you want a wake-up call for six o'clock?"

Gabriella said, "That would be fine."

"Do you want a bellhop? I have your usual room. I reserved the room next to yours for your friends."

"No thanks, we'll be fine. All we have is the clothes we'll be wearing tonight and a few small bags."

After they all took short naps, they walked together to the restaurant, which was only a block away. Jason and Dallys were there waiting.

After they sat down, Gabriella and Jason introduced everyone.

"My name is Jason, and this is my wife, Dallys."

Dick said, "That's an unusual name."

"My mother was a Dallas Cowboys fan, so…"

Dick said, "I'm an Eagles fan."

"Oh, I guess we'll be rivals then!" Dallys laughed.

Gabriella told them about their bet on the USC and Notre Dame game.

Dallys said to Dick, "You better know your roster—she probably had most of the USC players as students!"

Jason said, "That's enough about football."

"Gabriella, we haven't seen you since the funeral. How are you?"

"I'm on sabbatical at the moment, staying with my friends in Fort Lauderdale. After that, I plan to travel more."

"It's great to see you. Let's order drinks." He called the waiter over. "May I recommend our best wine, Philippe Foreau Vouvray Moelleux Clos Naudin 2009?"

Sue said, "I've had that before. It very good. I'll have a glass."

Jason asked the waiter to bring a bottle. "What can I get you, Dick?"

Dick said, "Do you have beer?"

"Of course! We have sixty varieties to choose from."

"Do you have Dogfish 90?"

"Sure."

"Tom, what can I get you?"

"Long Island Iced Tea, please."

"Of course. I hope not to sound too pretentious, but next to my family, this restaurant is the most important thing in my life. Gabriella helped us greatly when we adopted our daughter from Colombia about five years ago. Since Gabriella is from Colombia, she knew who to talk to."

He turned to Gabriella. "Will you have time to stop and visit Abigail? I know she would love to see you. She has become an excellent swimmer."

"Maybe Friday. Sue won the 200-meter freestyle in the 2000 Olympics."

"Fantastic! Maybe Sue can come also. That would be a thrill for Abigail."

Jason said, "This place is known for its stone crabs, but the tilapia is also very good."

Dick and Tom had the fish; the others had the crabs.

Dallys said, "So, how do you all know each other?"

Gabriella said, "Sue's my roommate. Everyone here works for a biotech research company and they are thinking of opening an office in Fort Lauderdale. Sue is a computer whiz, Tom has a master's in engineering, and Dick has the quickest reflexes of any person you'll ever meet. The company is trying to duplicate those abilities."

She turned to Dick. "Why don't you show Dallys and Jason some of your skills?"

Dick pulled three quarters from his pocket. "I bet you've seen someone put a quarter on the back of their hand, flip it, and catch it in their palm. But I can do it with three quarters." He did the trick. Dallys and Jason were amazed.

"I can do much more. I'm the best juggler you'll ever meet."

Gabriella said, "Believe it or not, this ability has great scientific importance if we can duplicate it."

After dinner, Dick went outside to smoke.

Gabriella said, "While we were shopping today, Sue and I thought of some things for Dick to do when he loses our bet. They're pretty funny—you want to hear them?"

Everyone said, "Sure!"

Gabriella said, "Make Dick dress up as a woman and walk up and down the block twice."

Dallys said, "I would bring my camera for that."

Sue said, "Gabriella thought of another one that's even funnier. Dick has to go to the gay beach and get a guy to come back to his hotel."

They all laughed. Dick came back from smoking. "What's so funny?"

Gabriella said, "I'll tell you later."

The waiter offered them after-dinner drinks.

Sue said, "We have to call it a night. We have to get up early."

Gabriella said, "This was great fun, and I promise that Sue and I will visit you and Abigail on Friday."

Dallys said, "Please do!"

They all said good night and thanked their hosts for a wonderful time.

As they walked back to the hotel, Gabriella said, "I hope Jason wasn't too presumptuous ordering the food and drinks. Our families have been visiting each other's restaurants, and the host always tries to impress the out-of-towners. Dallys and Jason are very nice, don't you think?"

Sue said, "Yes, I had a nice time, and I look forward to meeting Abigail."

******

The next morning, they had a tasty breakfast at the hotel restaurant. They were fairly tired, so there wasn't much conversation on the drive home.

Sue said to Dick, "Tom wants to practice his shooting this afternoon. Do you want to join us?"

"Nah, I've been practicing my whole life. Besides, there's a game on this afternoon."

He then said, "I'm cooking burgers on the grill. Would you like join us?"

Sue said, "Sure, after we practice."

Gabriella said, "I'm driving, so I get to choose the music." She tuned the radio to a song by Shakira.

Dick said, "It's not even English. What language is it?"

Sue said, "Spanish. Shakira is Gabriella's favorite singer."

"What does she look like?"

"Just like Gabriella. They could be sisters."

Gabriella said, "Shakira was also born in Colombia."

Back at the house, Sue had made a dummy to represent Mr. Cooper. She put a bag where the kidney would be. "It'll be about six inches above the rear end. You will pretend like you are drinking with a straw, which is really a syringe. When I tell you, blow the dart."

They practiced two times with kidney bags, then four times without. The first time, Tom missed the target completely. The next time, he hit it. All four times without kidney bags, he hit it right in the center.

Sue said, "Great!"

After they ate, Dick asked Gabriella what she thought.

"The burgers were a little overcooked. And you should have made a salad."

Dick got mad and told her she should do it herself the following week.

Gabriella said he could fix dinner next Sunday, but he just needed a little help. It was about eight o'clock, but since they had a busy week ahead, Sue and Tom went home early.

As they got ready for bed, Tom said, "When Dick loses the bet, he sure is gonna look funny in a Speedo!"

Sue said, "Let's have sex so that image is erased from my mind."

Tom said, "Sure. And thanks for a great weekend."

CHAPTER 4

TRAINING DAYS

In the song "Biko" by Peter Gabriel, he sings about apartheid, but its meaning could apply to the pro-embryonic stem cell situation. Since so many more people are getting involved, it is becoming a movement of its own.

******

It started as a pretty average day. Sue and Tom swam their laps. Dick and Gabriella did their workouts. Sue and Gabriella went to the office. Dick and Tom went to the rifle range.

After rifle practice, Dick, George, and Tom sat on the porch enjoying their cigarettes and drinks. A customer walked up who seemed out of place. Most people who came to the gun range were dressed in jeans and a t-shirt, but this guy was wearing an old suit jacket and a cheap pair of slacks. He looked like he hadn't bathed in a week, and he was very pale.

George whispered, "This could be trouble." He went inside to see what the man wanted.

A minute later, the men saw the guy point a gun at George. Dick grabbed Betty from his shoe, threw it, and hit the guy in the neck. George grabbed the man's gun as he fell to the ground, then checked his pulse to confirm that he was dead.

He ran out to the porch. "Go, and I'll tell the police I handled the robber myself. I want to help

Dick keep a low profile, so call me when you're in the van. I'll notify the police."

Dick said calmly, "Could you grab Betty for me?"

George said, "You start heading toward the parking lot, and I'll bring it to you."

They listened to the police radio in the van. Within a few minutes, they heard about an attempted robbery at Big Al's Gun Range. They listened intently for updates. The victim had been a known drug user, so the police assumed he had been trying to rob the club for cash and guns to sell.

******

That night at dinner, the robbery was the main topic of conversation. Dick wanted to know how many people knew about the pro-embryonic stem cell research movement.

Gabriella said, "Many more than you realize. Monty will tell you more tonight."

At seven o'clock, Monty appeared onscreen. "Over the weekend, we enlisted several people at the hospital to help. One nurse told me, 'It's hard to tell a soldier who lost his legs in Iraq that all we can offer him is artificial limbs.' The hospital staff has offered any help they can provide, so we decided to have Stu, Nate, and Mark help you out. Stu and Nate are expert marksmen.

"When Dick uses his blowgun on Mr. Peters, Stu will be in the room, so he can knock out the bodyguards. Nate will do the same for Mr. Cooper's bodyguards. They'll be wearing lab coats to blend in with the rest of the staff. Mark will also have your back in case anything goes wrong. If there are no questions, let's begin our practice."

Dick went first and hit the target well, but Tom did even better, hitting the same mark all three times. They used red and blue dyes to differentiate their shots.

Dick slammed his fist on the table. "DAMN. I can't believe Tommy Boy did better than me." He turned toward Pat and said, "Show me the results."

Dick added, "No weightlifting tomorrow, only shooting practice."

Gabriella said to the others, "I've never seen Dick so upset!"

Dick's whole world revolved around guns, so his ego was bruised.

******

On the walk back to their house, Sue told Tom, "Dick had a service dog named Max, short for Maxine. Max was Dick's loyal friend for twenty years. He loved that dog. One day, Dick tried to go

107

into a restaurant, but the owner wouldn't let the dog come in with him. He showed the papers stating she was a service dog, but the owner still refused.

"Dick had a routine of moving the wheelchair for two miles each night after dinner. He would always take Max. But the dog was getting old, and the two-mile run was too much for her. She died of a heart attack that night. Dick was not aware of Max's heart troubles, so he thought she had died because the restaurant owner had insulted her.

"At 8:45 that night, Dick went back to the restaurant. It was scheduled to close at 10:00, so he was the only customer. When the owner brought his food, Dick got Betty from his boot and killed him. As the owner was dying, Dick said, 'That's what happens when you fuck with me.' He then locked the front door, put the CLOSED sign up, and finished his meal. When he was done, he set the restaurant on fire. It burned to the ground.

"So you'll understand why Dick will be really motivated to shoot better than you tomorrow night!"

******

On Tuesday, Pat arrived at seven, and he and Dick practiced very hard.

Gabriella said, "I'll make you whatever you want for dinner."

Dick said, "I want steak and a baked potato— nothing fancy."

"Fine. Monty texted me this morning and said Sue and I should come to the gun range tomorrow in person to thank George. Is that okay?"

"Sure."

"Monty says that a personal thank-you is a valuable gesture."

******

If Dick was nervous about the practice that night, he didn't show it. He went first for target practice. The kidney is located above a person's behind; it's about four to five inches long, and six inches above the rear end. A perfect shot is needed to hit a kidney in the middle, infecting both the right and left lobes. Dick knew exactly where to hit.

After Tom took his shot, Dick made Pat show him the results. Dick and Tom had both hit the kidney, but it was obvious Dick's shot was better. Dick smiled and told Mark, Stu, and Nate about his and Gabriella's bet. Stu and Nate, who were also Notre Dame fans, said they wanted to come over to watch the game.

******

On Wednesday, Sue and Gabriella came to the range to thank George.

Dick said, "Good Old George—new shoes, new jeans, and a new shirt. If you had a new face, you'd almost look like a gentleman!" George gave him the finger.

Gabriella said, "George, I think you look very nice."

George told Gabriella he was happy with her reaction and he knew Dick well enough to ignore his comments.

Sue said, "We're here to thank you for helping Dick keep a low profile Monday."

"It wasn't that hard to convince the police that I handled everything."

******

Back at the office with Bob, Bill, and Pat, Monty said, "Other than thanking George personally, I had another reason not to have Sue and Gabriella here today. I love Sue like a daughter, but I don't think she'll be happy with what I have to say.

"If Mr. Peters and Mr. Cooper don't respond to our attack the way we want them to, we may have to follow another path—one that would result in the deaths of Tom and Dick."

Bob's mouth dropped open and he shook his head. "But that's unacceptable."

Monty said, "Yes, this alternative plan may be necessary because we want our actions to demonstrate the importance of embryonic stem cell research. On December 5th, Mr. Peters is scheduled to head an anti-abortion rally in Washington, DC. On that same day, Mr. Cooper will be leading another rally in Philadelphia. Dick will be in the house we bought, about 2,000 yards from Mr. Peters. He will fire a shot to kill Mr. Peters. Tom will do the same at that exact time in Philadelphia. Unfortunately, we'll also have to destroy the houses.

"We'll discuss this more on Friday. This weekend, we talked to a doctor, several nurses, and the head of maintenance. We would have talked to others, but we wanted to check their backgrounds first. The nurses will make sure the rooms are available, and I've been working with a construction company to install a firefighter pole in the closet. The doctor who will treat Mr. Peters and Mr. Cooper will advise them of three possible courses of action: start dialysis immediately, get on the organ donor waiting list, and check whether family members are able to donate kidneys.

"In the meantime, Dr. Jeb will be thinking that if the so-called pro-life movement hadn't seriously limited embryonic stem cell research, a fourth option may have existed. That is all for today. Please don't say anything to Sue or Gabriella about the backup plan."

******

While they were grocery shopping, Gabriella said, "I thought of another punishment for Dick when he loses our bet. You know how he's always giving me a hard time about my cooking? For a week, he'll have to make my 'fancy food' for all of us, following the cookbook exactly!"

Sue said, "Great idea! Plus, he'll have to eat all the food on his plate."

When they got back to the rifle range, George offered them drinks and suggested they sit at a table on the porch.

Gabriella said, "How long have you and your girlfriend been dating?"

"About ten years."

"If you don't mind my asking, how come you're not married?"

"We've both been married before. She wants to, but I'm not sure if I do."

"She won't wait forever. How long have you known Dick?"

"Oh, I guess about thirty years."

"Tell us a story about him that doesn't involve beating someone up."

"Yeah, there are plenty of stories about Dick hurting somebody. He's an angry guy."

Sue said, "We noticed!"

"Hmm. Okay, here's one. We were in this top-less bar. The girls were really friendly. We had a couple of drinks, and Dick said he could lift both of

115

them over his head. He bet them four drinks. Some other people even got into it. Before long, the whole bar was involved. Then Dick just pushed his chair over, grabbed them by the waist, and lifted them over his head, one in each arm!"

Just then, Dick and Tom returned from shooting.

Dick said, "Good Old George, always talking to the ladies."

Gabriella said, "He was telling us about the time you lifted two women over your head. Did that really happen?"

"Yes, you should never bet against me."

George got drinks for the guys, and everyone sat at the table. Gabriella never let Dick smoke in front of her, but she didn't say anything when George started smoking.

Gabriella told George about the bet. George said he would have to side with Dick for Notre Dame, but his girlfriend was from USC, so she would go for the Trojans. Gabriella, Dick, and George talked more about football, while Sue and Tom sat quietly and enjoyed their drinks.

******

On Thursday, all the talk was about the big bet. Gabriella had decided that Dick's punishment would be making dinner and eating everything on his plate for a week. No one knew what Dick had in mind.

Dick asked Tom, "What should Gabriella have to do if I win the bet?"

"Gabriella should let you smoke in the house."

"That's lame."

Gabriella announced her wager. "Dick, you have to make the dinners I want, and you must eat everything on your plate for a week."

Dick said, "I only cook hamburgers and hot dogs."

"Can you read a cookbook?"

"Yes, but my cooking will be below your standards."

Gabriella said, "That's okay. What's your task for me if I lose?"

Dick said, "This idea was on my bucket list: you have to put a dollar in every topless dancer's G-string while she's on stage at the local strip club."

Gabriella was so sure she was going to win the bet, she agreed to the terms.

Monday night would be a full dress rehearsal. Three people from the hospital would join them to judge everything. Dick and Tom did two practice shots each. Afterward, Gabriella invited everyone over Saturday for the big game.

******

On Friday, Pat helped Dick with his workout, but he said, "I miss my wife and daughters. I'm taking a plane to New York for the weekend as soon as we're done here."

Gabriella and Sue drove Pat to the airport. It was the first time Dick got to drive the van. Gabriella tried to show him how, but Dick got mad and said he had been driving for forty years and didn't need a girl to tell him how to drive.

Gabriella and Sue drove to Dallys and Jason's house. It was a three-bedroom ranch. They were surprised to see wheelchair ramps throughout the house. Dallys told them her mother had lived with them for ten years until she had died last year. She had been in a wheelchair for the last five years, so Jason had remodeled the house for her.

Jason had to go to work but had prepared a Waldorf salad. He asked Gabriella if she wanted a recipe for tilapia. Gabriella said, "Sure, I'll make it tonight."

Dallys introduced Abigail to Sue, and Abigail gave Gabriella a big hug. They had a big swimming pool, much like the one Tom and Sue had. Dallys already had the table set near the end of the pool, where they could watch Abigail swim. Sue ate her lunch but intently watched Abigail swim. After she was finished eating, she asked Dallys if she could swim some.

Sue got into the pool and asked Abigail if she wanted to swim a 200-meter freestyle. Even though Sue was over forty, she was still a pretty fast swimmer, but she only beat Abigail by three seconds. They swam a 200-meter race again; Sue beat Abigail, but just barely.

Sue said she was done for now. She then went to the pool house and changed. Abigail walked with Sue down to the table where Gabriella and Dallys were sitting. Sue told Dallys that Abigail was a very good swimmer.

Abigail said, "Mommy, can I have some Waldorf salad?"

Dallys said, "Go change your clothes and I'll get you some."

Sue said Abigail was very cute, but it was not a common Colombian name.

Gabriella said, "Abigail's mother was Colombian, but her father was an American serviceman. Both were killed by a Colombian drug cartel. Thank God Abigail was visiting a friend, or she would have been killed also."

Sue said, "That's a tragic story."

When Dallys and Abigail returned, Sue said, "I think Abigail's good enough to be an Olympic champion, but it would take a major commitment from all of you."

Abigail jumped up and down and squealed. "Oh my God, really? Mommy, did you hear that?"

Sue said, "Discuss things with Jason, and call me after the football game tomorrow."

Abigail said, "Mommy, please say yes!"

Dallys said, "I'm pretty sure Dad will say yes, but with all the swimming you did, you need a little nap."

When Abigail was in the house, Dallys asked Gabriella about the bet.

Gabriella said, "For one week, Dick will have to make the dinner and eat everything on his plate."

Dallys said, "I have a soul food recipe Dick would be sure to hate!"

Gabriella said, "It's time to leave, but we'll talk to you and Jason tomorrow."

******

Sue slept most of the way home. She had swum her fastest time in almost ten years against Abigail, but competing against a young kid had worn her out.

Gabriella talked about Pat's visit to New York. It was true he missed his wife and daughters, but also he knew that Sam had Parkinson's and had promised to help him explore retirement communities.

Monty had texted: "Special meeting tonight at seven. Look for a box at the house."

Sue was a little perplexed, but she trusted Monty completely.

Sue said she had to make arrangements for a breakfast on Sunday with an old friend. Gabriella had planned to make the recipe that Jason had given her, so she stopped to buy some fresh tilapia.

******

Later that night when Monty called, he instructed Sue to open the large box his courier had left earlier. Inside it were a number of smaller boxes.

Monty said, "Give each person in the room a box, but everyone should wait until I say to open them. After Tuesday, everything will be different. If anyone has a problem with that, please say so now."

The room was silent. Monty said, "Good. Everyone, please open the boxes."

There were seven very fancy watches.

"Dr. Bob, Bill, and I each have one also, and I gave Pat his this morning. The watches are very sophisticated. As soon you as put them on, a needle will puncture your wrist to measure your heart rate, your body temperature, and several other vital signs. The watches are synchronized, and you will use the second hand for several tasks. You should never remove these watches, even when you are bathing or swimming. Under extreme conditions, you will be able to hit a button to give yourself a lethal injection. We are hoping no one needs this function, but it exists. Are there any questions?"

Nobody said anything except Dick, "Well, this should be fun."

Monty asked, "Are you going to watch a movie tonight?"

Gabriella said, "We plan to see *K-PAX*."

Monty said, "Great movie, but Dick may want to opt out because nobody gets killed."

125

Mark said, "I have to go home."

Nate said, "I'm a recovering alcoholic, so if we go to a topless bar, I could be the designated driver." That sounded great to Stu and Dick.

Dick asked, "Can I call Good Old George?"

Monty said, "Sure, but no fighting."

Gabriella said, "I'll sleep in the extra room. You put Dick in the other room." Dick, Stu, Nate, and Mark left.

Tom asked Gabriella, "Do you worry about seeing Nate around alcohol, which might affect his recovery?"

Gabriella said, "No, Nate told us he was in the hospital for six months because he got drunk and wrapped his car around a tree. He vowed never to drink another drop of alcohol. That was thirty years ago, and he hasn't had a drink since."

******

Pat's wife picked him up from the airport, and they hugged and kissed for what seemed like an eternity.

On the drive home, Pat's wife said, "Sarah wants to come with you to help Sam tomorrow."

Sam had always made dinner, and his wife, Christine, made dessert. They had been a classic "10" couple. He was skinny, and she'd been a bit overweight, but she had a jolly laugh and was always positive, up until the day she died. It wasn't hard to see what Sam had seen in her. He never loved anyone more deeply.

Pat was happy with the work he did. He had sent three daughters to college, and they all understood that he had to work a lot. He said, "For a guy who just barely graduated from high school, I have a good life."

Pat had a wonderful night on Friday, but on Saturday morning, Sarah said, "You will see things today that will depress you forever."

The first retirement community they visited was the most reasonably priced. It was easy to see why. Outside most of the rooms, two people were sitting in wheelchairs. They were half asleep and looked like they hadn't bathed in days. The hospitals had dealt with the law stating residents could not be restrained in their beds by putting them in the hallway. That way, the nurses could keep an eye on them.

Sarah shook her head. "So sad." Pat agreed.

The next two places had three levels of care, each requiring increasingly more interaction from the nursing staff; therefore, they were more expensive. The first level was like the one seen in advertisements, active seniors enjoying retirement.

But most of the residents were in the second and third groups, which required additional attention. And most of these people were near death.

Sarah again said, "So sad."

After a depressing day, Pat said, "I want to go home and be with my family."

CHAPTER 5

THE BIG GAME

To say Gabriella was a football fan was a bit of an understatement. She was more like an unofficial coach. When she had taught at USC, she and Tim would record the games and have viewing parties every Thursday night. They had lived in an average-size house, but it had a large basement, which Tim had remodeled to accommodate the entire football team. The room had five large couches and a large flat-screen TV.

During her first year as a teacher, Gabriella had five members of the football team in her class and invited them over to watch games. She always made plenty of pizza. The students enjoyed themselves, even when Tim or Gabriella criticized their plays. She had two rules.

Rule One: If someone drank too much, Tim would drive them home.

Rule Two: During the game, they could only talk about football. If someone wanted to discuss something else, they had to go upstairs.

The first night had been a great success. The following week, the players had asked if they could bring their girlfriends. Gabriella always welcomed anyone, but they had to respect her rules. Sometimes the women would spend the whole night upstairs. Having the girlfriends there also fixed the problem of Tim giving players a ride home. Soon the whole team would come, so some people had to sit on the floor. Gabriella always sat on a pillow in a yoga position at Tim's feet. Most of the other women just stayed upstairs.

This had gone on for several years. But one summer, Tim started developing Alzheimer's, and by the fall, he was in a wheelchair. Nevertheless, the party continued. The players would carry Tim up and down the basement stairs.

Toward the end of football season, he was getting worse. Gabriella and Tim had a conversation that most people would find depressing. Tim had decided to end his life. As a psychologist, Gabriella could understand his reasons.

He got some pills from somebody he had worked with at one time. During the last game of the season, he asked one of the players to get him a bottle of water. He never told anyone else about his plans because he didn't want anyone to try and stop him.

Gabriella wept and hugged him. "I love you…"

By the time the game was over, Tim was dead. Gabriella called the police and coroner. One of the players and his girlfriend stayed with her all night.

Gabriella took time off from work, but she never got over Tim's death. The next fall, the football parties started again, but it just wasn't the same without Tim.

The football players always remembered Gabriella with great fondness. After she had made the bet with Dick, she had written to tell her friends she was interested in the USC/Notre Dame game. Players she knew from ten years prior took time off work to help the current players get ready for the game.

******

In the first quarter, USC scored seven points; in the second, Notre Dame scored ten. Dick was laughing and saying that he needed $50 in ones.

During the second half, Dick was cursing and throwing his shoes at the TV. Notre Dame got close but never scored. The first time, USC intercepted a pass; next, they missed a field goal; and the third opportunity, USC stopped them with their defense. USC scored twenty-one points to win the game, with a final score of twenty-eight to ten.

Dick said, "USC didn't beat Notre Dame; Notre Dame beat themselves. They had the ball inside the ten-yard line three times, but they couldn't fucking score. I think we should have another bet—double or nothing."

Gabriella said, "Are you trying to get out of our bet? I've already planned our first meal."

"Don't you feel bad not giving a guy a second chance?"

Gabriella laughed. "Not at all."

Dallys called to congratulate her friend. "Felicitaciones!" They both had a good laugh.

Dallys also wanted to talk with Sue. She had spoken to Jason, and he was interested in learning more about Abigail's chances of becoming an Olympic swimmer.

Sue confirmed Abigail's school schedule. "I'll be in Florida for a couple more weeks, but I have a friend who might like to coach her."

Sue and Tom went home early because they had a long day planned for tomorrow. Sue told him to just swim half his laps because they had to meet some friends in Miami.

They drove to a small Miami restaurant. Sue walked in and hugged her friend Cassidy.

Sue asked, "Are you and Nick still together?"

"Yes, actually we're engaged! When he finishes his residency in two years, we plan to get married."

They talked about how things were going.

Sue finished the conversation by saying she knew a young girl who was a great swimmer and that she needed a coach. She was wondering if Cassidy was interested.

Cassidy said, "I would be very interested in training a possible Olympic champion." She had some free time, so they drove to Dallys and Jason's house. When they got there, Jason answered the door. Abigail was in the pool, so they went out back.

Cassidy watched Abigail swim ten laps.

She said to Sue, "You were right!"

Jason told Abigail to come meet some people.

When Abigail got closer, she screamed, "You're Cassidy Flowers! Your picture has been on my wall forever. Daddy, she won gold medals in the 2004 and 2008 Olympics!"

Jason laughed. "How would you like Cassidy to be your coach?"

Abigail said, "This has to be a dream!"

Jason said, "It's real."

Dallys was inside watching football, but when she heard the excitement, she came outside to join the conversation.

Jason said to Dallys, "Please take Abigail inside and make her a sandwich." He started out by saying he had done some research and knew a little about the money required for Abigail's training.

They agreed that Cassidy and Nick would live in the bath house, because Abigail should swim two miles before school every day.

Cassidy said, "I thought I might waitress during her training, but I think training is a full-time job, so I'll need to give my current employer two weeks' notice."

Sue said, "I can coach Abigail for a week and a half until Cassidy can start."

******

Back in Fort Lauderdale, Dick was making hamburgers again, but this time Gabriella had marinated the beef overnight. When it came to food, Gabriella always made things a little more special.

Dick complained, "Now my all-American burger is a Mexican burger!" He tasted the home-made chips and salsa. He took huge bites and even asked for seconds. Under his breath, he muttered, "Wow..."

The next day's routine was quite different. Gabriella and Sue had a professional makeup artist color their hair and apply makeup.

******

Pat, Mark, Stu, and Nate arrived just before seven. Ten minutes later, three people who would judge the action arrived from the hospital.

Pat introduced everyone to Dr. Jeb Pine, Nurse Marlene Small, and Bob Hall, the head of maintenance for the hospital. Monty was on the closed-circuit TV as usual.

Before everything got started, Monty wanted everyone to guess which woman was Gabriella and which was Sue. The responses were pretty evenly split. Some people thought Gabriella was the nurse in a red wig, but actually that was Sue.

Gabriella had a brown wig. Monty was happy with the disguises.

Two teams were formed. Team A, Dick's team, included Gabriella, Nate, Mark, and Bob and would deal with Mr. Peters. Team B, Tom's team, would include Sue, Stu, and Pat and would deal with Mr. Cooper.

Monty continued, "We should show you our plan. Sue will act as the director. We will use Dr. Jeb and Nurse Marlene to pose as the bodyguards. Sue will cue the action."

Sue said, "Dick and Gabriella will start following Mr. Peters from the nurses' station until he gets near the room Nate is in. Mark will ask for his autograph. When he turns toward Mark, Dick will use his blowgun. At the same time, Nate will blow his dart at the bodyguard, and Pat will start the machine that shoots blanks. Gabriella will push Dick into the room, and Nate will lock the door." She told the people from the hospital to watch the closed-circuit TV, which would show them the action in the room.

"Gabriella will push Dick into the closet, where he will use the firefighter pole before her. Nate will unscrew the pole, then put a piece of wood and a section of carpet over the hole. Nate will exit from the adjoining room. Pat will stop the machine firing blanks."

Monty told the hospital staff that Sue and Tom would take similar actions with Mr. Cooper. "What do you think?"

Dr. Jeb said, "Sounds good. Since I'm the director of the hospital, I'll treat both men, and will inform you of their conditions."

Nurse Marlene said, "It seems like a good plan, but I think I should start the blank bullets, since someone might see Pat turning on the machine."

Monty told Bob, "You'll be busy on the lower floor. Pat will tell you what he's doing for Tom and Sue."

******

While Sue and Gabriella had their disguises applied, Pat, Dick, and Tom hung out in the backyard.

Dick said, "Do you want to hear about the time I spent in a VA hospital in Vietnam?"

Tom and Pat said, "Sure."

"I was wounded when I stepped on a land mine. For six months, I could only lie in bed. I had to use a bedpan. The guy in the next bed always complained loudly about the smell. I fucking hated

143

that guy." But I was only a sergeant, and my neighbor was a second lieutenant, so I had to keep my mouth shut.

"On the first day I got a wheelchair, I planned to make the second lieutenant eat his words. That night, I went over to the guy's bed, smashed tape onto his mouth, and shoved his nose and eyes in, killing him with much pain. The next morning, I woke to find that everything was cleaned up. I thought it had been a dream. Really, the hospital staff had known it would be bad press, so they cleaned everything up and told his family he died of an infection. So I got my Medal of Honor."

CHAPTER 6

HOSPITAL MISSION

At four o'clock, they all left for the hospital. While Gabriella drove, Sue applied bandages to Dick's and Tom's faces. Monty had Pat and Marlene fitted with communication devices. At 4:50, Mr. Cooper and Mr. Peters were done visiting patients. At precisely 5:00, they passed the nurses' station. Mr. Peters headed for the elevator, and Mr. Cooper headed for the stairs.

Gabriella and Dick started following Mr. Peters. Sue and Tom started following Mr. Cooper. When

Monty gave the signal, Pat and Marlene scratched their left knees with their right hands. Gabriella and Sue tapped Dick and Tom on their heads to signal that they should blow the darts. Nate and Stu blew their straws at the bodyguards. Next, Marlene started the machine that fired blanks.

Most people got down on the floor, but one security guard wanted to be a hero. He grabbed Dick by the shoulder, but Dick hit the guy with all his strength and knocked him out. Now they had a clear path to the hospital room. Once they were inside the room, Nate locked the door. Dick and Gabriella headed for the closet. Once they made their escape, the security guard shot the lock off the door only to find an empty room.

Down on the lower floor, Mark helped Dick remove his bandages and tossed them into a container full of acid. Gabriella removed her disguise and submerged everything in the container. Everyone left the hospital.

One last thing needed to be done: Bob had to remove all the tapes from the surveillance cameras and destroy them. He carefully moved the container full of acid and disposed of it.

Once outside, everyone headed for the van. Monty texted that everything had gone as planned and that they would have a meeting the following morning.

******

The next day, Monty informed the group that he had talked to Dr. Jeb, who had treated Mr. Cooper and Mr. Peters. Their kidneys had stopped functioning. Unfortunately, the men were being moved to another hospital, which was a nicer

147

place, but the new doctor said he would keep Dr. Jeb informed of their progress.

Monty said, "All we can do now is wait. I need to return to New York for about a week and a half, but I will talk to Dr. Bob and Bill every day. They will, in turn, keep you all informed.

"This will be the last day you will see Mark, Stu, and Nate, so you might want to have a cook-out tonight."

Later that day, Dr. Bob gave Monty and Pat a ride to the airport. Dr. Bob and Bill were invited to the cookout. Dr. Bob said he would enjoy coming, but Bill said he had some work to do.

******

Before Monty left for New York, he confirmed a dinner with his children. Monty wanted Pat, Pat's wife, and his three daughters to be there as well. After dinner, he had something to tell them.

Monty and Pat arrived in New York at four o'clock. Pat's wife picked them up. They had time to take a nap since dinner was planned for seven. Sam made Monty's favorite dinner of roasted chicken, baked potatoes, and corn. Dinner was enjoyed by everyone. All the girls and Monty's son had grown up together, and they were all good friends.

After dinner, Monty asked Sam to sit at the table. Monty said, "I recognized that you have the start of Parkinson's disease. You are a very important person in my life. Since I worked so much, you and your wife are the main reason my children had a somewhat normal childhood. I want to help you as much as I can."

Monty asked Pat's daughter, Sarah, since she was a registered nurse, if she would be willing to treat Sam at double her current pay. Sarah said she didn't need that much money since Sam was also important to her. Sam cried and accepted everyone's help.

Monty asked if Sam and Sarah wanted to return to Florida with him and Pat next week. Sarah wanted to give her current employer two weeks' notice, so she and Sam would fly down the following week.

Monty said, "It's time for bed for this old guy."

He asked if anyone would to like to run with him in the morning, and Sarah agreed to join him.

Monty said, "Good. Pat will drive us to Central Park at six o'clock."

******

On the way to the park the next morning, Monty asked Pat to text Gabriella with their plans. He would text Gabriella himself after he talked to Dr. Jeb. After ten o'clock, he called Dr. Jeb. After talking to him for some time, he decided Dr. Bob should talk to another doctor. He would then ask Dr. Bob to explain things to him in simple language. Dr. Jeb was okay with that arrangement because he had met Dr. Bob. Monty then texted this to Dr. Bob and asked him to call Dr. Jeb the following day.

Monty called Gabriella to explain his thinking and asked Dr. Bob to text her the next day. He then asked how things were going in Florida. She said everything had gone great the previous night. Even though she did not get to marinate the hamburger and chicken more than a few hours, the food had turned out well. The guys had smoked outside, but they did not drink. They played the game Risk until midnight.

Gabriella also texted, "Sue, Tom, and I are planning to go to Miami later today. Sue wants to meet Abigail's coach at school. I will text you tomorrow and let you know how everything is going."

******

They arrived about the time that swim practice started. Most of the kids were too young to remember Sue's time in the Olympics, but the coach was very aware of her history. She even knew that Sue's dad had died of ALS. Sue said she was just there to help Abigail and she would not get in the way. The coach replied that she would be honored if Sue would get in the pool.

Back in Fort Lauderdale, Big Al's Gun Range did not open until 10:00 a.m., so George offered to spot Dick while he lifted weights. After they were done, Dick went with George to the range. Gabriella said she would pick him up at about four o'clock.

Back in New York, Monty met with a group of gentlemen who were very interested in buying his company. Over the next week, Monty resigned from all the boards he was on and moved all his money to Swiss accounts. He called his son, Peter, in California and asked if he and Pat could visit over the weekend.

Pat's wife drove them to the airport. Monty was very nervous about seeing his son. Monty had been raised strictly Christian, and his son was gay. The last time they had seen each other, Monty had not been very understanding. He hoped his son would accept his apology.

The first thing Monty said when Peter picked him up from the airport was that over the past year, his beliefs had changed, and he loved him very much. His son and his partner, Ernie, were both successful actors. Monty then told him that Sam

153

had Parkinson's disease and planned to move to an island off the coast of China where they use embryonic stem cells to treat it. He didn't know when he would see Peter again.

Monty then asked whether Peter and Ernie owned their home. Peter said they were paying it off. Monty then offered to pay it all off. Peter said he would accept the offer since they were adopting a boy in a couple of months.

The first thing Monty did when he got back to New York was call Dr. Bob, who told him that Mr. Cooper and Mr. Peters were trying to find members of the Anti-Quality-of-Life Group who would donate kidneys. Monty was not surprised by this development.

Monday, Tuesday, and Wednesday, he finished moving all his money to Swiss bank accounts. On Wednesday night, he set up another dinner with everyone who had attended his dinner the prior week. After dinner, he offered to pay off everyone's homes. He said he hoped that nobody had made the same mistake he had of putting their job higher on their priority list than their family. Only when Sally had gotten sick and died had he wished that he had spent more time with his family.

On Thursday, Monty returned to Florida with Pat. He texted Gabriella that he and Pat would pick up Dick and Tom at the gun range.

When Dick and Tom saw Monty, they knew something was up. Monty told them that Mr. Peters and Mr. Cooper were going to forge the birth certificates of two members of the Anti-Quality-of-Life group so they could get new kidneys.

Monty then offered Dick and Tom $5 million each to shoot and kill Mr. Peters and Mr. Cooper. The only catch—and it was big one—was that they had to die in the process. If they agreed, Monty said they should think about who they wanted to leave the money to, iron out the details, and talk with Sue and Gabriella that night. They would meet for dinner the following night to talk about their decision. He wanted Dick and Tom to talk to the women separately because he thought their reactions would be very different.

******

Monty was right. Gabriella didn't say much, but as soon she saw them, Sue asked why Monty had picked them up. Tom told her he would discuss it with her after dinner.

When he told her what Monty had said, Sue was very upset. "This can't happen again. First my parents and now you. I'm going to talk to Monty and get him to change his mind."

Tom said, "No, I understand why it has to be this way. Besides, with my health getting worse, I will probably die within a year."

They discussed the situation all night, and Sue fell asleep crying in Tom's arms.

******

At Dick and Gabriella's house, things were very different. Dick told Gabriella what Monty had told him, then he said, "Life sucks."

Gabriella said, "I am unhappy about it, but I was aware that it might be necessary."

Then she said, "Do you want to watch a movie?" They decided the movie *The Crow* would be worth seeing.

Dick told Gabriella about his time in the hospital in 'Nam. Gabriella wasn't surprised.

Gabriella got a text from Monty asking if she could make a wonderful dinner for eight people the next day. She texted back that she would make boneless chicken over rice made with white wine sauce. Monty texted back that it sounded great.

CHAPTER 7

MOVING ON

Friday morning, Gabriella woke up first. She wanted go to the store to buy fresh chicken for that night's dinner. She asked Dick to come with her.

He said, "No way, most of the time I don't even go to bed until six in the morning."

She knew Sue needed to be alone with Tom. She was making Sue's favorite meal, and of course the chicken needed to marinate all day. You could buy the best chicken first thing when the market opened, so Gabriella decided to make the trip by herself.

At the other house, Tom got ready for his morning mile swim. Sue arrived at the pool, swam her mile, and was done by 7:30.

Tom asked, "Did you ever hear the Greek tragedy of Sisyphus?"

"I have."

"Having an incurable disease is similar to Sisyphus eternally rolling a boulder uphill then watching it roll down again, but there are three major differences. One is that Sisyphus was a bad guy. The second difference is that my condition is getting worse. Every year, rolling the boulder gets harder and harder. Third, my death will stop this eternal struggle.

"For years, I thought I would die after a meaningless life. Then you came along. I know I am going to die, but I want to be married to you. I guess that was one of the strangest marriage proposals you will ever hear."

Sue said, "Of course I will marry you! But there's something you should know. I'm pregnant."

After a second, Tom recovered. "You will be a great mother. Let's go back to bed…"

Sue said, "We can stay all day."

CHAPTER 8

THE FINAL DINNER

Monty said, "I need an answer from both of you."

Dick agreed, but he had one small request: he wanted to be buried with his dog's ashes.

"The ashes are in my apartment in Texas on the coffee table. You can have a key, but I don't think you need one."

Monty asked. "Who will the money go to?"

Dick wanted half to go to the Wounded Warrior Project and half to the Service Dog Fund.

Monty agreed, then he asked Tom, "What is your decision?"

"Since I have five brothers and sisters, the money should be evenly divided among them."

Monty agreed, saying he would have a fund manager deal with the money.

Then Monty said, "Let's eat."

Everyone was enjoying the dinner when Sue stood up and announced, "Tom asked me to marry him, and I said yes."

Gabriella was surprised. She started clapping and everyone joined in. It was agreed that since Dallys was a wedding planner, she would deal with all the details. Monty said they would work every morning and then they would join Dallys in the afternoon.

Sue said, "There's more...I'm pregnant!" which brought even more clapping from everyone.

******

The next morning, Dick and Tom went to the rifle range, and Dallys came to the office at noon to take the women clothes shopping.

Sue told everyone who was in her wedding party. She wanted Gabriella to be her maid of honor, Cassidy and Dallys to be bridesmaids, and Abigail to be her flower girl.

They went to the dress shop Monty had recommended. The usual time required to make a wedding dress was sixty days, but the owner said it be would be done in less than thirty.

Sue picked a white dress, and she, Gabriella, and Dallys were fitted for their dresses.

Dallys said, "I'll bring Abigail and Cassidy tomorrow."

******

Back at the gun range, Tom told Dick he wanted him to be his best man. Dick liked the fact that he would be in charge of the bachelor party. Sue had told Tom that Dick had to wear a tuxedo, whatever color Tom wanted. Pat had the job of picking them up since the women would be busy.

On the way home, Dick said that killing Mr. Peters and Mr. Cooper would be too easy on them. Instead, they should shoot them right above the eyes. That way, they would be in pain and require long-term care for the rest of their lives.

The next day Pat told Monty. He liked the idea, so they agreed it was the new plan.

Monty said that Dick and Tom needed to be on the second floor of the houses, so they should position their wheelchairs at the bottom of the stairs. If they rode up in an electric lift, there would be another wheelchair at the top of the stairs.

Monty also got twenty bodies from the VA morgue to confuse the investigation team when they looked through the wreckage.

******

Sue remarked how Dick had influenced Monty. This was a big ego boost for Dick. Gabriella told Sue that the smell of Dick's clothes reminded her of her father.

Sue said, "Do you love Dick?"

Gabriella said, "Love is not the right word, but he sure makes life interesting."

******

Plans for the wedding moved quickly. The next day, Dallys brought Abigail and Cassidy to the shop to be fitted for their dresses. There were plenty more details and so little time.

Sue tried to convince Tom to pick pink for the groomsmen's tuxedos, but because the dresses were white, he thought they should also be white.

******

Friday night came, and Gabriella said they would watch the movie *Freaks* by Todd Browning. She said it was a short film, only about an hour. Dick suggested playing one of his crude jokes. "I can get a salesperson to hang up on me." The phone rang, and it was a woman who sold timeshares. She was busy with a sales pitch when Dick asked her what she was wearing.

She said, "I don't think it matters."

Dick replied, "I'm not wearing anything."

The woman hung up.

Dick said, "She called me. I wanted to ask if she wanted to do FaceTime—that way, she could see me jerking off."

******

The following Friday, Monty said he had a surprise for Gabriella, and she told them all she had a surprise for Dick as well. The weekend went as usual, as Dick and Gabriella watched football and Sue and Tom stayed at their house.

The following Monday, Gabriella asked Monty about his surprise. He said she would have to wait. He would only tell her that they were going out for dinner. He wanted to know about her surprise for Dick.

Gabriella told them about Dick's bucket list item about her putting a dollar down every dancer's G-string. She said she would put a $20 bill down one dancer's G-string. She would do it for only one dancer, so Dick would have to make a hard decision.

On Friday, they all went to a fine steak restaurant. Monty predicted that Gabriella would criticize the food, and she did. She said the way she cooked steak was better.

Dick said he needed to use the restroom, so Tom went with him to make sure there was no trouble.

When they got to the restroom, some guy was talking on his phone in the handicap stall. Dick said he was going to cut the guy's balls off. The voice in the stall said, "Please put Betty away. Is that you, Dick?" The legend of Dick and Betty was well-known.

Dick said, "Yeah, and who the fuck are you?"

The guy said he was Ted Jones. "We fought together in Vietnam." He hurriedly exited the stall.

He said, "Normally, I wouldn't use my phone in a restroom, but my daughter is in the hospital having a baby. I thought it was an emergency." Tom noticed that he had a prosthetic arm. "I'm done. It's all yours."

Dick said, "No worries." Then he said, "How many children do you have?"

Ted said he had three boys and two girls. He could tell Dick and Tom were about to leave, but said it would be a great thrill for his kids to meet a real war hero. Dick was about to go out for a cigarette, but he said Ted's family was welcome to come over.

Ted came outside with his family and went on and on about how Dick was a war hero. Dick even had one of his medals with him. Ted took a picture of the boys with Dick.

After a while, Tom and Dick went back inside. Monty wanted them to blindfold Gabriella about two blocks from the music venue. Pat took them to a large room at the back concert hall. The artist started to sing, and Pat took the blindfold off so Gabriella could see it was Shakira.

Gabriella knew every song by heart. The surprise did not end there. Monty had arranged for Shakira to meet them backstage. Shakira knew everyone by name. She was even invited to Pat's daughter's wedding.

"Did Pat tell you about the Colombian statue I gave Sandra and her husband?" Shakira was amazed at how much she and Gabriella looked alike. They took a picture together. It was the best night of Gabriella's life.

******

Onto Dick's surprise. When they got to the strip club, everyone ordered drinks, but Dick acted like it was a big test. He had to pick just one woman, but he gave all of them a dollar.

After about an hour, he finally chose one. Gabriella was very embarrassed as she put the $20 into the dancer's G-string. They all cheered her on. They must have made a lot of noise, because a group of men started laughing and saying they wanted Gabriella to dance. Dick got mad and shouted at them.

Gabriella said to Dick, "You should think about whether you want to sleep with me tonight."

"You're right, let's get out of here before I kill someone."

They started to head out, but Gabriella said she needed to use the restroom. On her way out, she stopped at their table and said, "I just saved your lives."

One of them welcomed her to stay, but she said she needed to catch up to the guy she would be sleeping with that night.

******

Monday arrived, and the wedding plans started to take shape. Dick was Tom's best man, and he had asked George and Pat to be grooms-men. Everyone agreed on the white tuxes. The women dealt with the place settings and the invitations. It would be a small wedding of thirty people, including George's girlfriend, Pat's wife and his kids, and Monty and his family. But Monty, Dr. Bob, and Bill would all wear disguises. Sam and Jason were also invited. Sue and Tom had met three couples at the Unitarian Universalist church who would attend. They invited the people from the VA hospital. The only one who could come was Dr. Jeb.

******

It was Tuesday, and the men were sitting on the porch at the rifle range.

Dick said, "Hey, Tom, tell Good Old George about your experience with your neighbor."

Tom said, "I have the document that was read in court. Do you want to read it?"

My name is Tom Emerson, and I live by myself. I have a physical disability that keeps me wheelchair dependent. I do everything I can to live independently, but I have to rely on friends and neighbors to assist me with certain routine tasks.

One of those friendly neighbors was Jack Myer, who lived with his wife, Jill, across the street from me. He was a kind man who had a key to my home and helped in many ways. I returned those favors, for example, by helping to pay for some of their home repairs. I had known them for over ten years. Jill's brother, who I call Dracula, and his family moved in to help take care of Jack before he passed away.

Last spring, I was in the hospital for an extended period of time with a severe health issue. I thought it would be okay to ask Dracula to check on my home while I was in the hospital. During my hospital stay, I discovered that Dracula had stolen ten checks, forged my name on them, and cashed them in—a total of $1,788. The bank gave me the money back, and it will be Dracula's responsibility to reimburse the bank as part of his plea agreement, but no one will reimburse me for the frustration.

It was a disheartening and distressing event, and I am saddened by losing my trust in Jill as well. This event compounded my mental distress during my time in the hospital and made my return home much more difficult. After all this, I had to go through rehab. Then after returning home, I had another health incident that required me to return to the hospital. During this time, I worried about my home—it affected my sleep, my general feelings of insecurity, and my sense of how to manage my life.

I am extremely disappointed that Dracula is only serving probation for this violation of my home, security, and well-being. With the assistance of others, particularly from my church, I had to change many bank accounts and other services such as credit cards to protect my finances.

I hope this account will help the court understand the extent to which this event has negatively impacted me. I was very worried that the theft of the checks was not the only incident. And it was very time-consuming to get all of the potentially affected accounts reviewed and updated. It negatively impacted my recovery from the health issues *described above, and it has harmed my sense of security in my neighborhood.*

"Obviously, I gave him a false name. It made sense to use the name Dracula since the guy is a bloodsucker."

George said, "Then what did you do?"

"Not much. I was hoping the court would deal with it, but unfortunately they didn't do much. I guess he will just have bad dreams for the rest of his life."

George said, "Dick would properly kill the guy."

Dick said, "Not at first. I would break both his legs and, if he was living with Jill, I would break her legs also. The same goes for his wife, if she had the bad judgment to live with Dracula. As a matter of fact, I had a talk with a friend of mine named Steve and asked him to visit Dracula for me."

******

On Friday, Gabriella told them they would watch their last movie, *The Dead Zone*, based on the book by Stephen King. It had a meaningful ending where Christopher Walken sacrifices his life to save the lives of millions of people. Dick said their shooting the anti-stem cell people was a comparable move.

Gabriella said, "It's wrong to compare our situation to a scene in a movie that was based on Hitler's actions."

Dick said, "Really? Tell that to the millions of people who might benefit from embryonic stem cell research. The commitment President Kennedy made to put a man on the moon should be duplicated to find a cure for Alzheimer's by 2025. It is possible with embryonic stem cell research. The next president could go down in history as one of the greatest presidents ever. Every year, more than 300,000 people die who could possibly have been saved after more in-depth research."

After a heated discussion, Sue and Tom went home to bed.

******

On Saturday, Sue drove to Miami to see how Abigail was coming along. She was amazed by her progress. Abigail could beat her now.

On Sunday, Sue and Tom went to a Unitarian Universalist church and asked the minister to perform their wedding service. Afterward, they went to get tattoos, small ones on their ankles that read "I love you forever." The word *forever* held great importance for both of them. It symbolized life after death. They said their souls would be forever linked.

At five o'clock, they went to Dick and Gabriella's house for their weekly cookout, but they had football on the TV the whole time. Gabriella had marinated the hamburger all night in adobo sauce, giving the hamburgers a Spanish flavor.

******

Monday came, and the women went to the office in the morning, but the wedding plans were in full gear since the ceremony was on Saturday. Pat joined the men at the rifle range. George had a new friend with him. Since Pat was driving, he only had a Coke.

Tom needed to use the restroom. It was fully accessible, but he still managed to fall. He had used that restroom many times before, and knew he needed to hold on to the handicap bars before he got out of the wheelchair, but this time he didn't do that properly and ended up on the floor. He tried to get up but kept falling. He bloodied his arm, so he called for help. Pat came as quickly as he could and helped Tom get back into the wheelchair.

When they got home, Sue was concerned and called Dr. Bob to examine Tom. He was fine, so Tom just labeled it as one of those negative experiences he dealt with daily.

On Tuesday, Monty told them another part of the plan. After the wedding, they would all drive to Wheeling, West Virginia. There would be a van at a rest stop for Sue and Tom. So that would be the last time they would see Dick and Gabriella.

CHAPTER 9

THE WEDDING

The first wedding event was the bachelor party on Thursday. A brand new bus took them on what Dick called their "perversion excursion." There was a place for two wheelchairs and eight seats for everyone else. Dick had invited Pat, Good Old George, Monty, Dr. Bob, Dr. Jeb, and Sam. He had also invited Bill, but since he was a recovering alcoholic, he decided not to come.

Monty said, "Some people may think of Bill as being a little bit aloof, but don't think he isn't giving the movement his all." Bill was up most nights thinking of ways to make Tom's and Dick's actions more powerful. He had lost his wife to MS, and after she died, Bill did not want to live. He drank himself to a suicide attempt, which landed him in the hospital. The hospital had sent him to a recovery center. It was a nightmare, since most of the other patients were totally out of touch with reality. The unit was in lockdown, so he was not allowed to go outside.

After that experience, his whole life had been devoted to pro-embryonic stem cell research. Monty said there was no one who would want their actions to get the needed results more than Bill.

Monty said he would pay for everything. Dick wanted to go to Hooters for dinner. They had a nice waitress named Tayler. Dick ordered Dogfish 90. He said it was a full-bodied drink and only beer aficionados would enjoy it. He told all the waitresses that Tom was getting married in a couple of days.

Every place they went, all the ladies knew Dr. Jeb. Tom could tell this was not his first rodeo. At the first club, Dick wanted to see every dancer once, then they moved on to the next bar. At each bar, Dick wanted Monty to pay for a table dance. Dick wanted Tom to get a lap dance, so he watched each girl dance and then he made his choice. He said they would not leave the bar until Tom gave in.

"But Sue is the only woman for me!"

But Dick was insistent, so Tom finally capitulated. They went to three bars, and Dick had three or four beers each time.

Dick said, "You're all just lightweights!" Only George and Dr. Jeb kept up. This happened at all three topless bars. By the time they were at the last one, it was already 3:00 a.m.

The women had a bachelorette party, but they only went to one bar. When they got home, Gabriella said she would sleep in the other room. She said that she was okay with Dick being drunk and the fact that they had gone to topless bars, but the really bad part was that they had gone to White Castle where hamburgers are cooked in onions so Dick smelled bad.

******

The next night was the rehearsal dinner. All the people from the wedding party were there, as well as the minister, Anthony, and his wife, Iris. Tom and Sue talked about wanting to have their last name be Castleton.

Tom said, "It doesn't make sense to have our last name be Emerson, because I will be dead soon."

Monty had a surprise for them. He had hired the musical group Celtic Women to sing at the wedding.

******

The wedding chapel was impressive, with a row of windows where they could look out over a lush garden. Sue and Tom were happy that their friends from the church could join them.

Celtic Women sang "The Blessing" when Sue entered the church.

Sue and Tom had written their own vows.

Tom went first. "Before I met you, my life was empty. But every minute I am with you is a new high point. You have brought great joy to my life. I love you forever."

Sue said, "I was alone for years. My parents' deaths saddened me a great deal, but your love has healed me. I love you forever."

They exchanged rings and kissed.

******

For the first dance at the reception, Sue sat on Tom's lap while Pat pushed them around. They had chosen a song in which Máiréad from the Celtic Women played the violin. After that, a DJ played music.

A group of women were amazed by Dick's muscles.

George said, "In the past, you would have been all over them."

Dick said, "That was before I met Gabriella— no one compares to her. She is way out of my league; in fact, she's in a different ball field! She has me tied around her finger."

Gabriella had made a carrot cake for the wedding since she knew that was Tom's and Sue's favorite.

During the reception, Monty told Dick he was shipping their guns up north. He had bought another gun for Good Old George as a present. Monty said he would have it delivered to the rifle range Monday. George said it was a gift he would treasure for the rest of his life.

When people asked where they were going on their honeymoon, Tom told them, "We're going to Philadelphia." They would say, "That's a strange place for a honeymoon." Then Tom would reply, "It was the place we fought for our freedom."

It was the best day of their lives. Tom hoped his actions would pave the way for a happier life for future generations.

CHAPTER 10

ON THE ROAD

Gabriella said, "Monty wants you to go under-cover for a while after the shooting. Also, I'm afraid we'll have to get rid of Betty, because people might recognize the knife and figure out who you are."

Dick said, "Well, since I'm driving, I get to pick the music."

Most of the songs on Dick's CD spoke about vengeance because he thought the pro-life move-ment was responsible for stopping embryonic stem cell research. The second song was "A Mean Kind of Justice" by Carrie Newcomer.

He said, "It's a fucking thank-you to people who stop embryonic stem cell research and cost people their lives."

Gabriella said the people were just practicing their right to protest.

"I'm going to kill a few of them."

"You're crazy."

"There are other crazy people out there."

Gabriella said, "At the next rest stop, I'll drive for a while. Sue will cut your hair and trim your beard so people won't recognize you after the shooting."

Dick complained, "I've had long hair for forty years. First, Monty wanted to take Betty, and now you want to cut off all my hair."

Gabriella said, "You'll get over it."

******

The next day, they were on the road again.

Dick asked, "Do you want to see the new knife Monty got me? He knew how much I would miss Betty, so he got me another great knife. It's made of tungsten steel and is very sharp. I tried it out, and I throw it almost as well as I threw Betty. It's called Daughter of Betty. I want to put that on the handle, but Monty won't let me."

******

Sue played the CD she had made for her and Tom, which had several songs that meant a lot to both of them.

Gabriella said, "At the next rest stop, Dick is going to drive. And we're going to smoke some dope."

Dick said, "It's not fair. I can't smoke cigarettes, but you can stink up the van with your dope."

193

Gabriella said, "Okay, smoke your cigarette."

After they were high, Gabriella said to Dick, "It's not fair that we only smoked one joint while you smoked five cigarettes."

Dick said he needed to smoke more to deal with their stupid questions.

They got into a discussion about the war.

Dick said he understood why America had lost in Vietnam. "We were fighting on the wrong side. The Vietnamese weren't bad people. We were invading their homes and we had more fire-power, but they fought with everything they had."

******

The next morning, they were on the road again. This time they listened to a talk radio station. Some senator said he thought abortion was a sin.

Dick said he knew that the guy's son had been born with no arms or legs. The senator could not take care of him, so he had sent him to an institution. The senator and his wife visited him every other Tuesday and half days on holidays. One Christmas, the mother had asked her son what he wanted. He told them he wanted hands, so he could wipe his ass. People said the senator was brave by not encouraging his wife to have an abortion, but his son said he was just a dumbass, and he would have to live with his dad's bad decision.

When they stopped, Gabriella said it would be their last dinner together since the next day they would be splitting up.

******

On the last day of their journey, they stopped at a rest stop about ten miles from the hotel. Monty had them change vans there because there would be surveillance cameras in the hotel parking lot.

Everyone was sad knowing they would never see each other again. The goodbyes were emotional. Gabriella, Sue, and Tom hugged each other, but Dick just shook Tom's hand. He would never hug another man.

After their goodbyes, Sue and Tom left for Philadelphia. Gabriella and Dick were fairly close to Washington, DC, so they stopped at a truck stop, where a group of men checked out Gabriella.

When Dick and Gabriella got ready to leave, two of the men sat down in their booth and held a knife against Dick. They told him they would all take a trip to the parking lot. Gabriella was taken by the other two men. Dick went with them because he did not want to cause a scene in the restaurant.

Outside, one of the men complained about why he had to do the dirty work, while the other two got to enjoy the woman. Dick muttered to him-self that they would meet a sharp-dressed woman called Daughter of Betty soon.

The other two men had taken Gabriella back to the restroom. One of the men said, "You go first, and I'll hold the gun, Dale." In true redneck style, Dale said, "That's very white of you, Dennis."

Gabriella reached into her purse, which was designed by Bill with a small hole for the video camera. She started recording. Back in the park-ing lot, Dick decided to make his move. He needed to kill them fast to get back and help Gabriella. He grabbed the Daughter of Betty from his boot and went for the guy's neck; at the same time, he took the knife from the other guy and went for his neck, too.

After they were both fatally stabbed, Dick moved his wheelchair as fast as he could back inside the restaurant. He got a rag from a bucket, wrapped it around his hand, and used all his strength to break down the restroom door. He threw the Daughter of Betty into Dennis's neck.

Then Gabriella used some moves she had learned in kickboxing. She kicked the guy in his balls. When he went to grab himself, she kicked him in the head, knocking him out. She got everything on video. Gabriella pushed her button to alert Monty.

******

Monty's men came and acted like they were police officers. They said they wanted to take Dick and Gabriella to the station for questioning. When they were out of sight of the restaurant, they let Dick and Gabriella go. One of the fake police officers stayed back at the restaurant so he could talk to Dale, the head of the truck-stop jerks, when he woke up.

Dale told him that Dick and Gabriella were trying to rob them. Gabriella had left her phone behind, so the officer played that for the guy. When he got to the part where Gabriella kicked the guy in his balls, the officer said, "That must have hurt." The officer asked the man if he wanted to come down to the police station and give a statement, but when they were trying to get him into their car, he ran off.

******

Dick and Gabriella headed to Washington, DC. Dick called Sue and Tom to tell them what had happened. Dick laughed about how Gabriella had kicked the guy in the balls. Gabriella corrected him and said she had kicked the guy in his "private area." Everyone had a good laugh.

After a while, Sue and Tom got into a conversation about his job. He told her that in less than a year, he had gone from walking to using a wheelchair. He had made what he thought was a dumb decision, but really he had been experiencing a nervous breakdown. After talking to a woman he knew in Boston, he had bid for a position three levels lower than his current level at the time. The people at work didn't understand what a drag it was to lose his ability to walk. Tom thought the manager should have called his doctor out of concern or encouraged him to see a therapist, but unfortunately he didn't do anything. Tom took the position but was forced to retire after a couple of years.

Sue said, "Life has not been kind to you."

"Someone once told me I should have said something. But when a person is having a nervous breakdown, they don't really think logically. The people at my company really lack compassion. My life has been stranger than fiction. It was unhappy for many years. But then you came along, and everything changed."

******

After stopping for Chinese takeout, they arrived at their final destination. Sue wanted to call Gabriella, but Monty said they should not use the cell phones anymore, so she called from the land-line. Gabriella said she planned to leave at seven o'clock. Monty wanted them to refer to the shooting as "the party." So Gabriella said she needed to go to the store to get ready for the party.

After dinner, Sue and Tom went to bed early because they wanted to listen to their CD a couple of times. The first thing they talked about was the baby. Sue had seen a doctor, and she knew it would be a boy. She wanted to name the baby Tom. He told her he would only accept Thomas, and anyone who called him Tom or Tommy should be corrected. He also told Sue he wanted her to get married again because he thought it was good for Thomas to have a father.

Sue said, "You are his father."

Tom said, "He needs a living father."

The first song on their CD was "My Heart is Low" by Mary Black. Sue had listened to this one the most, and every time she would cry. She knew reality required Tom to die, but it did not make it any less painful.

The second song was "The Island" by Dolores Keane. Sue said she listened to it every night before she went to sleep, because in her dreams Tom was whole again. The third song was by Mary Chapin Carpenter, "The Calling." It reminded Tom that the pain and suffering he had gone through had a purpose.

As they listened to each song, they were aware this would be their last night together, but they hoped Tom's actions would help people see the need for embryonic stem cell research, which could help future generations live happier lives. They fell asleep.

In the middle of the night, Tom heard Sue leave, but he didn't say anything because everything had been said the night before.

CHAPTER 11

THE PARTY

Thoughts From the Author

I have suffered and felt so much pain, which might explain my actions. By stopping embryonic stem cell research, the pro-lifers cause me pain. They must pay for their actions. It is hard not to be bitter when the doctor says, "We wanted to help you, but the pro-lifers say abortion is a sin, therefore limiting embryonic stem cell research."

******

Tom woke at about eight o'clock. Sue had left him a plate of food. She had also left a note: *I love you forever.*

Tom got up and took a shower. The "party" was scheduled to start at eleven. The TV was set on a station that showed the rally in Washington, DC. As Monty had planned, there were twenty bodies placed throughout the room.

Tom wanted to listen to his and Sue's CD a couple of times. He called Dick and they talked about the wind conditions. Tom told him there was a flag on stage he should use to aim the gun, which they called Party Popper. Dick was very aware of how he should aim. He said he was going to watch the news to see if anything had changed. They synchronized their watches.

Dick wanted to call Tom a good junkyard dog, but Monty had told them not to use that expression, so he just said, "Good luck."

Tom said, "All life is sacred." His own life had been a nightmare, from the time in Florida in his twenties when he had become aware of his disability, his ability to judge distances had started to fail, and he hadn't dealt well with it. The next forty years had been a time of sadness, until he had ended up in a wheelchair.

So he thought the expression "All life is sacred" was a bunch of bullshit.

The first three songs on the CD were mentioned earlier. People say when they are doing an activity, songs play in their head, which motivates them to perform better. With Tom, he swam faster. During times when the songs referenced dancing, he replaced it with swimming.

The fourth song, "I'll Be Where the Heart Is," reminded Tom that their love was not done.

The fifth song was "Imagine," which reminded them to see that with research, it could be possible to end the waiting list for organs. The research would also help them to better understand and treat all forms of cancer.

The sixth song—the Indigo Girls' "The Girl with the Weight of the World in Her Hands"— speaks of a person who does not hide the pain she feels.

Tom said to himself, "I wonder if more bad things will happen to me. The list seems endless already. I have an illness that is getting worse. I need a wheelchair. My neighbor stole my checks. A crazy woman named Linda who had been a good friend for ten years told people I was stalking her. After that experience, I went into a deeper depression."

******

Thoughts From the Author

With my disability, things are worse than they would be with so-called "normal" people. Like the problem with Linda. I was already depressed when I called my friend in Boston, but her response sent me into a deeper depression. It darkened my life for the next fifteen years.

Another example can be seen in my dealings with Dracula. After spending a month in the hospital, I went to rehab. I was only supposed to be there for two weeks, but then I discovered the problem with my bank account. People would tell me, "You can't go home, because your neighbor is stealing your checks." So I had Dracula to thank for keeping me in the hospital another month.

I have talked about the frustration of having to cancel and change all of my credit cards, which was more difficult because I cannot write or speak well. I am lucky that I had some good friends who helped me.

******

At 10:50, Tom got ready to take his shot. They had planned that the shot should be taken at exactly 11:00. Monty had not told them this, but the two other guys were to shoot at 11:05.

Before Tom had shot Mr. Cooper, he knew the fate that awaited him. He knew that millions of people would benefit from embryonic stem cell research. Like the woman who was just informed she had Alzheimer's and whose future looked bleak. Or the guy who learned he had Friedreich's ataxia and was told he might not live past thirty.

Tom took his shot and hit Mr. Cooper above the right eye. Tom hoped this man might experience the hell that he had known his whole life. He watched the TV screen, but Dick did not fire his gun. Tom called Sue, who said there was a closed-circuit TV monitor to show Dick. He had had an unexpected visitor. He had killed the guy with the Daughter of Betty, but the guy had got a shot off, and it had knocked Dick out of his wheelchair.

Sue said that he had until 11:04 to take the shot. She saw on the monitor that Dick got back into his wheelchair, took a shot, and hit Mr. Peters. Dick then threw his gun to the other side of the room.

Tom's last deed was to push the button on the watch. Monty said that at 11:10 the bomb would go off, so they should be dead by then.

******

Sue's and Gabriella's actions were precise. They left the command center at the same time in two separate vans, which had license plates right out of James Bond—a revolving mechanism displayed new plates. They drove the vans to remote locations and changed cars. People were assigned to drive the vans to a junkyard, where they would be destroyed. The two women took shuttles to separate airports and flew in different directions to their final destinations.

Monty and Bill were the only ones who knew where they were going. In case anyone was looking for two women leaving the country, Bill had planned for them to meet children at the airports to throw off investigators.

Once Sue was on the plane, she began to listen to the first song of her and Tom's CD, "A Woman's Heart," and wept for most of the trip.

Sue listened to that CD several times a day every day during her pregnancy and went into a deep depression. Monty knew that Dr. Bob's son was a good friend of hers from childhood. So he arranged for him to visit her. It turned out that Dr. Bob's son, Chris, was a doctor practicing Obstetrics and Gynecology. Once they met, Sue lit up. Dr. Chris was told that Tom had died in an auto accident.

Later, Dr. Chris delivered Sue's baby and eventually they married, but she never forgot Tom. Every June 22 (Tom's birthday), Sue would spend some time alone. Her husband would always take Thomas camping.

The next chapter of Gabriella's life went a lot smoother. She was at peace with Dick's death. Gabriella was so wonderful that she met a man and got married within a year.

Monty, Pat, and Dr. Bob dealt with Sam's Parkinson's disease.

Once Thomas was born, Sue was a lot happier. Dr. Chris was a good husband. The following year, she had a daughter and they named her Gabriella. Sue wrote Gabriella to tell her. She started out by telling her about the news she had read in *USA Today*. The article was titled "Man Dies of Gangrene of the Scrotum." It stated that a man named Dale had suffered with an injury for many years after he had gotten into a bar fight.

Sue told Gabriella how she had married Dr. Bob's son and they had named their daughter Gabriella. If anyone called either of her children Tom or Gabby, she would correct them.

The letter was short because Monty did not want her to go into much detail about the mountains or the nice weather. She ended the letter by saying she had seen Abigail swim in the Olympics.

Gabriella wrote back, saying she was honored to have a girl named after her. She believed Dick's spirit was still at the site of the shooting, so she had asked Dallys to go there and tell him that the Eagles finally won a Super Bowl. She went on to say that she had also gotten married, and they had adopted two children from Cambodia.

******

Sam and Pat's daughter, Sarah, joined Monty in Florida and went with them to an island near China. Sarah ran with Monty every morning. She ran much faster than him, but she always ran alongside him for the first mile, so she could tell him about Sam. Sarah would run ten miles in the time it took Monty to run five.

Sarah was very close to the doctor who treated Sam. They had a lot in common: they both believed in embryonic stem cell research, and they were both avid runners. They were engaged to be married the following year. Monty then had two runners to tell him about Sam.

Sam was treated for his Parkinson's, but unfortunately the disease had progressed too far, and the doctors said embryonic stem cell research had progressed too slowly.

******

Thoughts From the Author

Because of pro-life positions, we are functioning at about a 15 percent ability to save people; with more research, we could have possibly functioned at 90 percent.

If you believe in embryonic stem cell research, write your congressperson or state representatives and tell them how you feel. If you are able, please donate to the National Ataxia Foundation.

This book is fictional and should be seen as such. The premise of harming or killing pro-lifers is as repugnant as pro-lifers killing abortion doctors. Terrorism even for a higher purpose is hard to defend. All violence in this story is intended to create a suspenseful murder-mystery drama and is not to be an endorsement of any real violence. It does, however, symbolically reflect the frustration of so many who suffer.

I believe in nonviolence; therefore, I took a lot from Gandhi's statement when he was talking to a general in the British Army. It is not logical to think that one million people from Great Britain can govern fifty million people from India. I say to the million pro-lifers: People who might benefit from embryonic stem cell research don't think that an embryo's rights are more important than theirs.

THE END

REFERENCES

Program in Stem-Cell Biology and Regenerative Medicine, University of Florida, Shands Cancer Center, Gains

ACKNOWLEDGMENTS

I would like to thank several people who helped me with this book. To help pay for editing and publishing, I used a GoFundMe account.

I am very grateful that my sister Nancy and her husband Michael Bounds told several people about my need.

Dan and Karen Laughman also told several people, plus Dan read the manuscript and gave me feedback.

I would like to thank David Levitt, who helped with several grammatical errors. In the early stages of the book, both Noel Olson and Mike Arenson helped with many comments.

I would also like to thank the college student volunteers from Lori's Hands, a nonprofit organization founded in Newark, Delaware, that connects students with individuals in the community living with chronic illness. For many years, the students have made dinner for me and visited me at home. One goal of Lori's Hands is to help students understand the experience of living with chronic illness. Many of the students who visited me through Lori's Hands have asked me about my health and about ataxia. Sometimes, they would read drafts of chapters of this book aloud to me and we would discuss my writing and my experiences. I always enjoy their visits and benefit a great deal from them. I know several other people who have had students from Lori's Hands, and everyone loves the program. Thank you to the many students who have visited me, including Eliza, Gunther, Katelyn, Tara, Kim, Alexa, Mary Kate, Sam, Alyssa, Adem, Ashley, Leslie, Tyler, Parker, Philip, Lola, Cooper, Jennifer, Victoria, Ian, Joey, Sydney, Alexa, Erin, Kristen, Austin, Maura, and Kyla. Lola in particular was so interested in my writing and my life experience, and had a great memory about things we'd talked about in previous weeks. Ashley made me a Thanksgiving meal and joined me for dinner. It was the first Thanksgiving that I shared with friends in 40 years.

My neighbor Ron and his wife Cathie Kelly were a great help in many ways. Ron, as well as Brandon and Katie Toole, showed me how good neighbors can be. Dallys Holland, Brittany Riddle, and Joan read the book and talked about each character. Joan even said Dick was likable, and she enjoyed Gabriella's love of food. Jeb Haslam commented on editing.

I thought my English grammar was too bad and I didn't think I had anything to say that people wanted to hear. But a lot of people read the manuscript and gave me encouragement. Two of the most important people are Sarah Miesner and Cass. I met them through another program at the University of Delaware called Yes U Can Corp, co-founded by Vickie George. The program assists adults with disabilities with exercise. I worked with them from the time they were freshman until they were seniors. Sarah read the book and told me how much she liked it. Joe Rupert was a great help, as were Ruth Jobes and Wayne Wilson.

My good friend Tim Kelly wrote the foreword.

A friend asked me to autograph a book for her. After many years of using a wheelchair, my hand is cramped, so I use a rubber stamp for my name instead of signing.

Thank you to Sheila Younger, Becky and Bob Varlas, Christopher and Erin Knight, Dave and Ginger Emerson, Jane Baskin, Megan Gilimore, Pat & Joanne Kane, Mike Kiesle, Kyle Bryant, Pat Wisniewski, Bob Lilllich, Bob Benson, Michelle Mills and Paul Smith, Steve Goodwin, Steve and Ginger Nobles, Sam Dobbs, Stuart Abelson, Yun Yang, and Paul Weaver. Thanks to George Cullin for letting me use his nickname, Good Old George. I would like to thank Mary Pat Curry and Nancy for being great sisters. They wanted to support their brother by buying the book. Mary Pat and Nancy were there when I dealt with hard times as well as good times.